MIKE SPEARS

REASON WHY I SING

Author's Bio

Mike Spears, the true definition of multi-talented. Coming from the small impoverished community of Pembroke, Illinois has seasoned Mike with a keen humble spirit that's destined for success. Landing a major recording contract with Universal Music Group, Mike has proven himself as a singer/ songwriter. Leading him to perform and appear on major networks like; MTV, BET, VH1, and FOX. After a few singles failing to chart, and a fully un-released album Mike found himself at odds with life and the music business. Taking a hiatus from the music business to literally travel around world as an Entertainment Host for a cruise line has kept him busy for over three years now. While traveling the world, Mike took out time to write about his life and experiences as a recording artist in this book titled *Reason Why I Sing*. To protect the identities of those involved in his musical experience, Mike turned what was supposed to be a no-holds-barred tell all story about his experience and life as a signed artist, into a fictional drama-filled cautionary tale. With great reviews before its' official release, *Reason Why I Sing* marks a new beginning for Mike Spears.

PRELUDE

Firstly I would like to thank you, yes YOU, for taking your time to read my story. This story has haunted me so much that I had no choice but to write it. I had to come clean with myself. Writing this story was by far the hardest thing I have ever done in my life. I am exposing a lot about myself. I become completely naked and allow my flaws to show in this story. I've lived a life where I have pretended to be more than I was, till one day I was sick of myself. I had grown annoyed with who I was because it was fake and lacking substance. This story has honestly saved me from myself. I feel free. I feel like I am on my way to finally being the person that GOD has called me to be. So I have *no choice* but to be brave and stand in my TRUTH. GOD is *true* and I aspire to be just as the spirit of GOD.

This story is based on my real life situations. These are some of the things I've encountered while trying to make it in the music business. I have changed everyone's name (including mine)to protect people's identities. I didn't want to incriminate anyone. I changed some location and company names as well. But the story and lessons are all real. This story actually takes place over the course of six years in Atlanta. I've met so many people along the way that has helped me get to my goals; some celebrities, and some everyday people. I've encountered more people that tried to take advantage of my talent though. But regardless, all of them had something to do with the *Reason Why I Sing*...ENJOY!

WARNING

Though this work is based on real life events and situations, it is a work of fiction. Names, characters, places and incidents are either the product of the author's imagination or are used fictitiously, and any resemblance to actual persons, living or dead, business establishments, events or locales is entirely coincidental.

-Spearit Publishing

Reason Why I Sing – Track Listing

TRACK 1: Lose Yourself..........1

TRACK 2: Down Low (Nobody Has To Know)..........18

TRACK 3: Same Love..........23

INTERLUDE: For The Open Minded..........25

TRACK 4: Sweet Dreams..........30

TRACK 5: Ready or Not..........39

TRACK 6: When Doves Cry..........49

TRACK 7: What's Goin' On..........56

TRACK 8: How Do You Like Me Now? 65

TRACK 9: Welcome to the Jungle..........72

TRACK 10: Waterfalls..........80

TRACK 11: We Need A Resolution..........86

TRACK 12: Love You Forever..........95

TRACK 13: It's Not Right But It's Okay..........105

TRACK 14: I Ain't Mad At Cha..........110

TRACK 15: They Don't Care About Us..........121

TRACK 16: Don't Stop Believin'..........125

TRACK 17: Mo' Money, Mo' Problems..........136

TRACK 18: When It All Falls Down..........148

TRACK 19: Dance With My Father..........160

TRACK 20: A Change Gon' Come..........168

TRACK 21: Ain't No Sunshine..........176

TRACK 22: Livin' On A Prayer..........183

**BONUS TRACK: Reason Why I Sing..........189

TRACK 1:
Lose Yourself

I can't believe I've gotten to this point in my life. There have been plenty of times I felt like I wouldn't make it. I'm a cocktail of emotions and problems. I've been sexually and mentally manipulated, molested, abandoned and left for dead. I've been stripped of all my dignity and pride. Coming from an impoverished community, trying to live the life of the "rich and famous" to make others proud and happy left me with nothing. The little confidence I had has been traded in along with my soul for a chance at stardom. Many have wondered; what shall it profit a man to gain the whole world and lose his own soul? Absolutely nothing... Read on...

Thank God I'd finally arrived. Sitting in Atlanta's early morning downtown traffic on a Friday should've been the least of my worries before another audition. Pulling up to "Build-A-Star Rehearsal Hall and

Studios" I could barely find a place to park. I decided to park in a parking garage which was only two blocks away. Build-A-Star was a popular location for people that worked in the entertainment industry. The best of the best have rehearsed or recorded there. I said a little prayer before I got out of my car. As I walked up to the "Build-A-Star Rehearsal Hall and Studios" two-story white building, I could hear a sea of different voices singing loudly. I guess they were warming up their vocal cords before they head into the audition. I wondered if I should do some type of warm up. I didn't want to seem over confident, even though this had to be the hundredth audition I'd been to since I'd moved to Atlanta two and a half years ago. I took my place behind the last person in line, which was right outside the doors to the building. I began to hum a little bit of the song "Blackberry Molasses". Humming would at least keep my throat warm in this late January weather. Just as I began to sing a little bit of the chorus under my breath, the guy in front of me turned and asked, "What song is that?"

"Blackberry Molasses," I replied.

He quickly asked, "By Mista?"

"Yes, it's one of my favorites," I replied.

"Mines too," he said.

After that quick exchange, he reached to shake my hand and said, "My name is Marcel."

"I'm Juan," I replied.

From there we discussed what brought him all the way from Washington D.C. and what brought me all the way from a small town not far from Chicago. We both came to Atlanta for the same reason, and that was to pursue a music career. Atlanta was the place where lots of unknown talent was being discovered. It was known as the Motown of the South. And even though I was in my junior year of college, getting an education wasn't my sole purpose for coming to Atlanta. Getting my education was just an excuse to move away from home.

Finally, we made it inside the building and out of the cold. There were still at least a hundred guys in front of me in line. In the lobby of this rehearsal studio there were posters of Atlanta's top selling R&B/ Pop boy group, Last Horizon, which is the reason I was there.

After going platinum on their first album, their lead singer, Leo, quit the group and they were having auditions to replace him. Last Horizon had won two All Star TV Awards and a Grammy nomination from their self-titled debut album.

As I looked around the room I had begun to daydream and wonder. Why after so much success on their first album would the lead singer just give up and quit? I actually had their album and the lead singer sang on every song, even the talking parts. I wondered if he got a big head and the other three guys decided to kick him to the curb. He must've had the Eddie Kane Jr. syndrome.

"We are looking for confidence, SWAG, and personality," the guy holding the mega phone yelled as he woke me from my daydream.

Marcel turned and asked, "Are you nervous?"

"Umm, just a bit I guess", I said as I wiped my sweaty hands on my jeans.

Walking along the long line of guys, the guy holding the mega phone announced, "You will only get one minute to sing whatever song you have prepared. This is your one and only shot. Whomever we choose today will be called back for a second audition in which you will be asked to dance. Good Luck!"

`As I turned around I could see more guys filling up the room. Now I began to get extremely nervous. Even though I considered myself a professional when it came to standing in lines to audition, my palms were soaked with sweat.

Two hours had passed and I was about second in line. Marcel and I talked the whole time and had exchanged numbers. We actually planned to go watch the Super Bowl at a sports bar in Atlantic Station on Sunday. Atlantic Station was a newly built outdoor shopping complex located a couple miles from downtown. Though I'd been in Atlanta for a while, I had few friends and Marcel seemed like he'd be cool to hang out with.

"NEXT," the guy on the megaphone yelled to Marcel.

"Do your thing man," I said to him as he walked through the door. It was the point of no return. I was now also nervous for him as well as myself.

Moments later I heard Marcel singing, which sounded really good to me. He stopped abruptly, as if someone had cut him off. Seconds later, he walked out the door with confusion and disappointment written all over his face. As he quickly passed me he whispered, "Good Luck."

Seeing Marcel's expressions made me want to get out of line and go home. I got that butterfly feeling in my stomach and I felt as if I couldn't breathe.

"NEXT," the guy yelled for me.

As I walked into the room I saw the three remaining members of the group—Cal, Matt, and Kev—a middle-aged big black man, and a woman sitting behind a long table directly in front of me. The tension in the room was so thick my body began to feel heavy. They all looked unwelcoming and tired from doing these auditions. All their eyes looked upon me as if I wasn't worthy to be in their presence.

"Name," the lady asked rudely.

"Juan and I'm from Chicago," I replied.

Even though I'm not from Chicago exactly, I usually tell people that I am. It's close enough...

"Alright, Juan, let's hear what you can do," she said with a shrug.

In that moment I completely blanked out and gave it my best shot. I opened my mouth and began to sing and perform. Though they made me extremely uncomfortable, for some reason I found my home in that feeling. I usually did my best when I was uncomfortable.

I made it through the verse and chorus when the big guy raised his hand and told me to stop. "Juan, right?", he asked.

I nodded nervously.

"How long have you been singing?" , he asked.

"Since high school, so about 5 years," I said.

"We want to see you again tomorrow, here at 1 p.m.," the lady said.

With the biggest smile, I said, "Okay, I sure will."

"Thank you," the guys in the group added.

I walked out of the room feeling like I just won a million bucks. Even though nothing was official, it felt so good to at least have the opportunity to show up the next day. I thought, even if they didn't pick me for the group maybe they could still hook me up with a record deal.

For some reason just having a record deal satisfied a lot of artists, including myself. Getting a record deal is honestly not the hard part. The hardest part is keeping the record deal and being interesting enough for the record company to invest time and money into your projects.

I know lots of artists who have and are signed to major record companies, but will never get their records out in the stores. But being a bit ignorant to the music industry and how it worked at the time, just having a record deal was like a certificate of success to me. I just thought once you get signed to a record deal you get a million dollars. With that million dollars you'll buy a house and nice cars to show off in your music videos. Then life would be great from then on out.

As I got back to my car I checked my phone and saw that I had a text message from Marcel asking how it went.

I immediately replied, "Great, man, they want me to come back tomorrow for the second audition!"

He replied, "Oh, man, that's what's up. Congrats! Let me know how tomorrow goes. Are we still on for Sunday?"

"Thanks, and most definitely," I replied.

When I got home that day from the audition I was filled with excitement. Since I knew the next step in the audition process was dancing, I went to YouTube and studied all of Last Horizon's music videos. To be even more prepared, I practiced doing their routines in the videos, as well as singing all of their old lead singer's parts (which was the entire song).

While studying Last Horizon's videos I realized that they reminded me of the boy group HB3 (Heart Break Three). Their lead singer also sang all the parts on their songs including the backgrounds. When you look at the credits on the album you'll see that they give credit to different background singers. It's very similar to the whole Milli Vanilli ordeal.

At the time I didn't understand why they needed background singers if they have a group of singers. Now I understand that the other guys are normally just there to complete the image of the group. They don't have much musical talent at all. They can be groomed to be photogenic; thrown in the gym to get nice bodies; dressed up by the stylist; coordinated by a well-known choreographer; thrown into a studio with a famous producer, engineer and Auto-Tune; presented to the right record company with the right amount of promotion and stars are born. It's all about marketing.

Their target market is young high school kids, and those same kids could care less who is actually singing on which song. They're more concerned with what the artist looks like. Juicing up the image of the artist makes them more appealing to their target audience regardless of what they may actually sound like.

Arriving at the second audition was even more nerve wracking. When I walked into the rehearsal studio there was pure silence. It was nowhere near as loud and crowed as the other day. There were two other guys sitting on a bench outside the same door from the day before. As I approached them, I asked if they were here for the second auditions and they both nodded and said, "Yes."

They both looked just as nervous as I was. I reached out my hand and said, "I'm Juan".

"I'm Jason."

"And I'm Mark," the two guys said as they reached to shake my hand.

I could see now that they wanted a certain look for the group. These guys looked similar to me; about 5'11, athletic build, medium brown complexion. It made sense since the other guys in the group were all about 5'11 and athletically built. They were all in good shape. After waiting for about ten minutes, the lady that was in the audition room yesterday came out to greet us.

Then she explained, "As you know, you're here to fulfill an extremely important role in Last Horizon. These guys have won awards and even been nominated for a Grammy. Of course we are looking for a guy that possesses the look, the voice, the moves and the charisma. We have already begun the recording process on their second album. We need someone who is hungry for this. We need all of your time, focus, and dedication. If you feel like this is something you can't do, I ask that you leave now and not waste your and our time. Now follow me."

Neither one of us said a thing. We all just nodded and smiled. She led the three of us into the rehearsal studio where we auditioned the day before. Sitting behind the table again were the guys in the group and the big black guy. Standing to the right against the wall filled with mirrors was "Swerve". Swerve was a famous choreographer that worked with the biggest of the biggest musical acts, including HB3.

"They're all yours, Swerve," the lady said.

"Okay, fellas, I'm Swerve and I'm going to start off showing ya'll a quick eight count."

He proceeded to show us the routine. About four steps in; I began to realize that these are the steps to the group's first single, "On My Mind". I started to feel a bit relieved because I practiced these steps while watching the video the night before.

After he finished showing us the routine, he said, "Alright, now we're going to try it with the music." He pressed play on the sound system and as the intro to the song played he yelled, "And five, six, seven, eight," giving us the cue to start.

Without thinking, I breezed through the first eight counts. I could tell the other two guys were struggling with it. They would stop and look at me to see the next move. I felt grand at that point.

Growing up, I was picked last when it came to sports. When I was in Elementary and High School I shied away from anything that called on me to be athletic. But in this arena I thought I was the Number One Draft Pick. I'd trained and practiced every day for this moment. Seeing them struggle with the routine made me feel bad for them, but this moment was mine and I wasn't going to dumb myself down. I started to imagine me on stage with the group performing for thousands of people.

After about thirty minutes of going through the entire routine, the lady instructed us to go through the entire song individually with the guys in the group. She pointed to me and told me I would go first.

Cal, Matt, and Kev all stood up at once and took their positions. One stood a few feet directly behind me, one stood diagonally to the right behind me, and the other to the left diagonally behind me. From a bird eye's view, we were in a diamond formation, just as I had seen it in the video. I felt powerful at that moment. I felt like this was mine. I felt like I had made it already.

Swerve pressed play on the sound system and counted us down, "and five, six, seven, eight."

I lost myself and became who Leo was to them. I nailed every step and sang along louder than the song so they could hear me. After I finished, it was the other guys' turn and they both were really good. I started to second guess my performance.

After they both finished the lady stood to say, "I want to thank all three of you guys for showing up today. We are going to discuss a few things and we will contact you if we believe you can take the group to the next level."

As the other two guys turned and walked out the door, I went to the lady and shook her hand and said, "I'm sorry, but I didn't get your name."

She said, "I'm Teresa, the group's manager." She gave me half of a smile.

I then told the guys in the group "Well, whatever decision you guys make I wish you the best and I still will continue to support your music."

They all looked at me sincerely and nodded. Then Kev said, "Thanks man, we really appreciate that."

I knew my tactics may come off as brown nosing to some, but hey, I wanted this bad. And I wanted to stand out from the other guys that auditioned.

Later that evening as I arrived to my apartment, I received a call from the group's manager. She told me right away, "We would like for you to be the new addition to Last Horizon."

My heart pounded so hard that my body began to tremble. As she kept talking, I could barely understand what she was saying. I was so excited that my mind couldn't wrap around the first thing she said.

As I collected myself she asked, "How do you feel?"

With the loudest burst of excitement I said, "Thank you, thank you, thank you." At that very moment I felt my entire life shift into a new direction. Into the direction I always dreamed of, but never knew how or when it would happen.

She proceeded to tell me that my first rehearsal with the group was on Monday night, and I would be on a probation period before I signed any contracts. Monday would be perfect since I had classes in the morning. I could definitely understand a probation period, but I was so excited I wanted to sign those documents that night. I've dreamed of these moments my entire life and I was all in. *Nothing* was going to stand in the way of me and my dreams.

After the conversation with Teresa I was on a high. I called my mom and cried to her and reassured her that our lives were about to change. I thought to reach out to my father but I didn't think he'd care. I told everyone else I knew that was close to me about this great news. I even texted Marcel and told him. He was excited for me and reassured me that we were still on to hang out on Sunday to watch the Super Bowl, and to celebrate.

For the rest of the night I could barely think of anything else but what was about to happen to my future. How would this affect my relationship? How would this affect my friendships? How would this affect me? Little did I know this great dream of mine would turn into a nightmare I never anticipated.

TRACK 2:
Down Low
(Nobody Has To Know)

On Sunday I went down to Atlantic Station to meet with Marcel like we had planned. He told me once again, "Congrats on possibly joining Last Horizon." I could tell that he genuinely supported me even if he didn't get it.

After watching the Giants beat the Patriots 17 to 14, Marcel invited me back to his house for a couple beers and to catch a few highlights from the game. Thinking nothing of the friendly invitation, I accepted and followed him to his home, which was close to Bankhead.

I rarely went to this area. It's not as bad as people may have described, or maybe because I'm from the hood it didn't seem as threatening to me. Marcel lived in an upscale townhome which looks out of place. I followed him inside where he proceeded to give me a quick tour of his house. The entire house smelled like Pine-Sol, which reminded of home. His furniture was all white suede, on top of thick fluffy white carpet. I've never experienced carpet this soft. I could sleep with no pillow on his floors. I asked him how old he was, because I wondered how someone my age could afford to live in something that seemed so expensive. He told me he was 29. I was a bit shocked because he looked like he was around my age, which was 20.

"Dude, you look very young, not saying you're old," I laughed.

"I know I get it all the time, I drink lots of water and eat lots of healthy stuff," he explained.

"Well I have to get like you, man. So what do you do to afford a home like this," I asked.

"Well, both of my parents are doctors back in D.C. They help me out a lot, and I work at a clinic in downtown Atlanta" he explained.

"So where's your girlfriend? I know you can't keep the girls off you," I jokingly said.

"Well my girl is out of town for some convention, I guess. So you got a girlfriend," he asked.

"Oh yeah, man, definitely, something like that I guess," I shamefully said.

"What do you mean? Are ya'll not getting along," he asked.

"Right," I answered quickly.

We eventually ended up in his living room to watch the highlights of the Super Bowl. I sat in his recliner, which faced away from a staircase and the rest of the house, but toward the TV. He laid down on the couch, which was to the far left of where I was sitting. During more conversation, we cracked open a few beers. We talked and laughed on and on. It felt like I've known him my entire life.

He got up from the couch and said he had to go take a piss from drinking all the beers. As he got up and walked away I begin to wonder if I could drive home. I was a bit tipsy.

After about three minutes of waiting for him to return, I felt two hands from behind me begin to stroke and massage my shoulders. Feeling confused, I jumped up quickly and turned to look. "Whoa man, what are you doing," I asked.

"What's up, man?" Marcel whispered seductively, giving me the low sexy eye.

My pulse began to race as I instantly became nervous. This is one of those moments that I've heard about in movies, where a friend comes on to another friend of the same sex. Though I always thought my reaction would probably be different. It was so unexpected because Marcel is about 6'0, light brown skinned, with hazel green eyes— the model type of guy that could have any girl he wants— but he was coming on to me. Shocked but intrigued, I went along with it.

I lay back where I was as he slowly massaged my shoulders. He whispered, "What's up? Let's go to my room." I agreed and followed him upstairs.

Afterwards I felt guilty. I thought Marcel would be a good friend but this could make things awkward between us. I know Atlanta is filled with DL (down low) dudes but Marcel is someone I would have *never* suspected.

"Are you okay?" He asked as I grabbed my car keys to leave.

"Yea, I'm good," I replied. But I lied. I wasn't good. The guilt I began to feel was strong. I just cheated. What would this do to my relationship? How would David feel if he found out?

TRACK 3:
Same Love

The ride home to College Park seemed to go so fast. My mind was pre-occupied with what just happened. Just as I walked into my apartment my phone rang. It's David. From the conversation I felt as if he knew I'd just cheated. Or, maybe it was my own guilty conscious. I had been with David since I came to Atlanta. We met on "Blackworld.com" months before I moved there. Though the relationship was serious I always considered myself to be bi-sexual. This was something I knew as a teenager. I still was attracted to women and had desires to have sex with them.

Meeting David was one of the best things that happened to me in Atlanta. David was 5'7, with a small athletic build, caramel colored skin, and big innocent eyes— definitely worth the scrutiny I might face if others found out about my sexuality.

He was softer than I but a very decisive, professional, by-the-book, and no-cutting-corners type of individual that researched *everything*. Extremely analytical. He was the type of person you wanted on your team when you need to get things done. Our personalities conflicted at times because I'm more abstract in my decisions. I'm a dreamer and David would've much rather had a 9-to-5 and work his way up in a company. David was also in college.

Though we'd definitely had our ups and downs, nothing like cheating ever came up before. I never thought I was capable of allowing that to happen. But it did. Even when I gave David the news about me joining the group he was the only person that didn't take it so well. Though he was happy that my dreams were possibly becoming true he didn't want it to come between us. I reassured him that it wouldn't.

I knew that I would have to keep our relationship a secret if I wanted to go far in the music industry. Being "gay" just doesn't go so well when you're supposed to be entertaining women, especially in the urban community. There have of course been rumors of gay or bi-sexual men in the music industry but I never really bought into them. I always put it in the back of my mind. Regardless, I knew my relationship with David meant a lot to me but not more than my dreams.

INTERLUDE:

For The Open Minded

Growing up I always longed for a relationship from a masculine source. My father wasn't really around much so I was primarily raised by my mother, grandmother, and aunties. Not having my father around much as a kid I always felt less than everybody else. I felt like I didn't matter. I felt I wasn't good enough to be his son. So I did everything in my power to get his attention. I figured at a young age that if I got good grades in school my father would come to pick me up and we'd spend time together. I got good grades and he still didn't seem to care.

I remember crying a lot growing up. I would go off to myself and cry for what seemed like hours. I just didn't understand why he didn't love me, especially how he loved his other children.

One time in the midst of my tears and sorrow, I seriously contemplated committing suicide. I thought that if I killed myself maybe my father would come to my funeral just to show he cared. What was it about me that made me unworthy of his time and attention?

When I went off to college we didn't talk for over a year. By that time I had just about given up on the possibility of us having a father and son relationship. I started to live life for what I knew it to be. I never wanted to use the fact that my father was absent from my everyday life as an excuse for my sexuality.

Growing up as a Baptist, hearing that I'm going to hell because of my sexuality was motivation for me to build a relationship with God, myself. I didn't accept what I was being taught in the church so I withdrew myself. I feel like God is our creator and he created us in the image of love. And the love that I was created in wasn't what I felt in the church.

I was taught to fear God and never to question Him. I don't believe that God should be feared; why should I fear what created and loves me? I believe we should question God when we don't understand. He built us with the ability to question and I use it all the time. I don't feel like God has punished me in any way for it. As a matter of fact I believe I've gotten further in life questioning God. When I ask God why, the answers are revealed to me. I'm then able to move on with understanding without carrying any form of fear. So many people are afraid to ask God why, but asking often produces answers. When answers are produced, we then have a better understanding.

Some may say my sexuality is an abomination, an automatic ticket to hell. I think it's quite amusing how people think they know what God hates or dislikes. (Please don't say, "It's written in the Bible".) As if they've interviewed God for themselves. I'm who I am because God made it so. I prayed and fasted hard for years begging God to change my sexuality and desires but praying didn't work. So to say that praying didn't work is the same as saying, "God isn't real". I refused to believe that God wasn't real, so I grew to accept who God made me to be. I look at it as if it's a gift, not a curse. I love love, no matter where it's coming from. If God is love and love is God then that's where I want to be. I can't tell you what the future will bring, but I know I'm where I suppose to be in my life.

Do I believe I'm going to hell? Absolutely....not... Firstly, I don't believe in such a place. Hell is a mythical place that doesn't exist unless you create it. The human psyche is a much more powerful tool than we give it credit for. What we believe is what we ultimately receive. Believing your life is hell, creates more hell for you to live in. I like to believe that I'm living in heaven right now. Everything around me is perfect because God made it so. What is just is. Even when things happen in my life that may be perceived as "bad", I know God's intentions aren't bad. God allow obstacles to build faith and love, not to cause harm.

Ultimately, I believe in just being a good person and spirit. Many of us make decisions in life based off what other's may think and feel about us. We allow our egos to take control of our thoughts and make decisions for us. In most cases we always find ourselves stressed trying to keep up with the image that we've allowed our egos to paint.

Connecting to the spirit we'll find that nothing on the earth really matters. In the spirit we become weightless and detached from the rules and laws that bounds us to the earth. We can see through the eyes of our very own hearts, which just wants to love. There's no stress because there's no fear in the spirit. The spirit doesn't have the ability to fear what others are going to do and say.

Being spiritual allows me to do good things for people even when they may not deserve it. The good deeds we do for other people allow them to be happy even if it's just for one second. That second of happiness may change their life in the most dramatic way allowing them to potentially change millions.

Our only responsibility in life is love. In life we are presented with challenges everyday that makes it extremely hard to see any love. Our faith is constantly being tested. The good part is that we only have two choices and that's to love or hate. It's easy to simply ignore those challenges, but they'll pop up all the time if not confronted carefully.

Choosing to hate, takes so much energy that it could ruin other potential good things in your life. Choosing to LOVE isn't always easy but it definitely feels better within. Just accepting life as it is and embracing every moment is easier than resisting life itself.

God is so cool because he's able to love unconditionally. God's love for his creations is more than a million times a mother's love for her only child.

I find it funny that people think God is sitting somewhere on a throne in the midst of clouds eating grapes, with a long white beard. God isn't male or female. God doesn't have to be, he just is. I say "He" because we have been programmed this way our entire lives. As humans we give everything human-like characteristics to help us better relate or understand it. So for us to understand God we have given him human like features.

Sorry but God is not sitting somewhere with a penis. Why would he need one? So you tell me that God has to step off his throne to go pee? God just is. We are sometimes very simple-minded when it comes to God. God cannot be described physically. We don't possess the understanding or vocabulary in any human language to describe something as magnificent as God.

I choose not to be religious because I feel like God created me strong enough to live free. I'd much rather be free to think of my own possibilities. God created me to have a mind that imagines beyond what I see, so I take advantage of that gift. There are some people that need the guidance and structure from religious institutions. They need to be guided back to the love of God.

Sometimes the world can be so distracting with its problems that people forget their way home back to God. I'm not against religions because they all seem to have a common purpose and that's God. Many people have died trying to prove their God is God. God is often used against people to gain control over the weak spirited. God is God, beyond all human fantasies. God is everything we need. It's not my place to tell you how to live your life. I believe the greatest of all religion is God. Our purpose is to get to the spiritual state that he's in, which is love.

Just a fun human example: Wal-Mart is a supercenter where you can pretty much get all you need to live. Just because you didn't ride in my car don't mean you can't find your way to Wal-Mart. You may take the bus marked "Christian", "Muslim", "Buddhist", "Jew", etc., but we all will get there to get what we need. On every bus there are different rules. Some buses you can't chew gum, drink, smoke, talk, sing, or even sit, but that's up to you to figure out which bus best suits you on your journey to Wal-Mart.

Whichever bus you choose you must follow the rules or be judged by other riders, or even be put off the bus. Then you'll have to walk to Wal-Mart, which is okay because you'll get a chance to experience the journey of life for yourself without the guidelines that have been set by religions. Whichever way you take, make sure you find a way to get there and get what you need to survive, which is God.

TRACK 4:
Sweet Dreams

The next day after class I met with David at a café before I went to

my first rehearsal with Last Horizon. Out of all the times we'd spent

together, that time was different. I felt dirty. I felt like I was deceiving him

and myself. As much as we'd been honest in our relationship, I knew I

couldn't tell him what happened between me and Marcel.

"So how did last night go with your new lil friend you met at the

audition?"

"Oh, good… He's really cool, really good guy," I replied.

I felt like David was on to me, but then again he always asked questions.

"We all should hang out one of these days," I said. I'm not sure why I just let that slip out of my mouth. I'm so notorious for putting myself in those awkward situations.

"Yea, that would be good. I would love to meet him. Any friend of yours is a friend of mine. Right?" David immediately replied.

"Absolutely. Well, let me get ready to head to rehearsal," I proposed, quickly changing the subject.

"Yea, call me afterwards, maybe I'll come by tonight," David replied slowly, as if he was unsure.

Leaving David there at the cafe felt so different. For the first time I felt like we may not survive. I started to really consider how much Last Horizon would be the last of Juan and David. But I couldn't think about that, I had to put my game face on for the rehearsal.

During rehearsal I was being taught all the choreography for Last Horizon's show. Swerve wasn't being so nice about teaching me anything. I figured he knew how serious this situation was and he couldn't take it easy on me. Cal and Kev both were very supportive; they would pat me on the back every now and then. Those moments made me feel great because there was so much pressure coming into this position. Matt, on the other hand, seemed very distant. Even when I attempted to make conversation with him, he was very short with me. He wouldn't even look me in the face. But I couldn't allow that to distract me from this great opportunity. I figured he'd eventually warm up to me. After going over choreography for about three hours, the big black guy from the audition walked in with a keyboard. By this time Swerve had already left us alone to rehearse.

"Alright fellas we're going to go over some vocals," the big guy said.

I walked over to him to shake his hand and ask him his name.

"Maestro is my name but the fellas call me Stro", he said. "How's it going so far?"

"Good; lots to remember, but I'll get it," I replied.

Stro was actually really popular in the music industry. I have never seen him but I've definitely heard of him. He wrote and produced songs for some of the top acts in the business. He also owned Build-A-Star Rehearsal Hall and Studios in which almost every artist to make it big from Atlanta attended. Record companies know that Stro is a great coach and any artist he had developed was definitely Star Quality.

"Alright fellas, we're going to go over the vocal warm ups," he announced. All four of us huddled around in front of Stro and the keyboard. Now I had got a chance to see where the rest of the guys were vocally.

We began the warm ups and it became apparent to me why Leo sang every song on their album. Matt and Kev seemed to be at least able to hold a tune which is okay for some background vocals. But Cal seemed to be almost tone deaf, though he was able to blend in with the rest of us, sometimes at least. After about 30 minutes of going over some vocal exercises, Stro instructed the other guys that rehearsal was over for them and they were free to go home, but he wanted to go over more things with me.

After they left, Stro began to play a slow ballad on the keyboard. I realized it was the last track on Last Horizon's album, "Tears". He tells me to sing along.

As I was singing he told me to perform the song. He told me to feel the words of the song and show more emotion. Since the song was about doing all you can in your relationship so there are no tears, pulling my emotions out shouldn't be so hard.

After a few attempts, he started to give me pointers. He explained to me that this is the fan's favorite song and closes every show, so it was important to deliver. He told me at the climax of the song I should rip my shirt off to help ignite more emotions and screams from the fans.

"So strip," he said.

I nodded to agree and got ready to give it another try.

"Strip," he said again.

Looking confused I asked, "Take my shirt off now?"

"Exactly," he said demandingly.

Feeling so uncomfortable, I slowly took my shirt off.

"So what was so hard about that," he asked.

"Oh nothing, I..." I stuttered. He began to play the song again and told me to sing the song to him as if he was a fat ugly girl in the third row. He told me to make her feel special. I did as he asked and it seemed to be working. He continued to play, nodding to let me know I was doing well.

At the climax of the song, he told me to get on my knees and crawl. In my mind I'm thinking this was way too weird but I did as instructed. At the end of the song, I rose to my feet.

"Have you ever messed around with a guy?" He hesitantly asked me.

"Umm no, never have and never desired to," I said firmly. I wasn't about to admit to anything of that caliber at that moment.

"I could swear you meant what you were singing just a second ago," he said.

"Oh, you told me to sing to you, right? So I did," I said with a laugh wanting this moment of awkwardness to end.

"I'm definitely not into dudes, but the way you just sang that to me... that's how you want everyone to feel when you're on that stage. You want them to think it's about them," he said.

"Oh thanks," I replied, still feeling a bit lost because I wasn't sure what he was getting at.

"Okay, try it again, but this time I want you to take your pants off," he said.

"I'm sorry but I don't see...okay," I said.

"See, you'll never be a good artist. Maybe this isn't for you. You have to be willing to do *anything* for this. How you think Leo did it?

Remember you're not officially in the group, you're still on probation," he said.

Thinking about my life, the relationship with my father, and how much I really wanted this, I began to unbuckle my belt and slid off my jeans.

"Alright, now take off your underwear," he said.

"Okay I'm not comfortable with that, man," I said forcefully.

"See it's my job to break you, to get you to think differently, to push you to the next level. You already took off your shirt and jeans. You sang to me like I was a chick. What's taking your underwear off going to change now?"

Thinking that I've told everyone about me joining the group, I didn't want people to think I was a failure or even a liar, so I took off my underwear. Standing there naked I felt stupid. I felt like I was losing a part of myself.

"Alright, now this time I want you to stand right in front of me and sing," he said. I stood in front of him but he instructed me to come even closer. He told me to sing the song acapella.

I began to sing to him as he admired my naked body. He reached his hand up between my legs, grabbing my inner thighs. My voice trembled and my body was flushed with an instant chill. He then stood and took out his piece and began to pleasure himself.

"You say you want this, right? Don't let one little moment take you away from your dreams," he said as he continued to pleasure himself.

This moment caused me to mentally shutdown, my clear judgment was off. I felt like I'm that six-year-old boy again being molested, wanting my father to rescue me. Not understanding that it's wrong, but knowing it isn't right. I felt disgusting. I felt like I was being humiliated. I hoped God wasn't watching.

TRACK 5:
Ready or Not

About two weeks later I received a phone call from Teresa while I was in class. She said that it was important that I made it to her house as fast as possible. I left class immediately because this, my dream, was way more important than school at the time. Teresa told me that they needed to have an emergency meeting with me at her home in Alpharetta, Georgia. This would be my first time seeing where she lived. She texted me her address, I pulled it up on Map Quest and was on my way.

I knew this had to be something serious since she was allowing me to come to her home. The entire way there I rehearsed every song I could think of. I just wanted to be prepared in case they were going to have me sing for them. I knew this had to be something good and I was excited for whatever it would be.

As I pulled up to the gated manor, I visualized myself living in one of these two-to-four million dollar houses. I figured if I worked hard enough in the group for at least two years I'll be able to easily afford one of my own. Clearly my perspective of the music business was off.

In her long drive way I saw one red Ferrari, one Mercedes truck, and two black Audis. Driving a 1999 Chrysler Sebring, I was immediately humbled. When I got into the house I was greeted by Kev and he led me to an all-white conference room where I saw the rest of the group, Teresa, Maestro, and two other professionally dressed black women.

"Hey, Juan, come on in and have a seat," Teresa said excitedly.

I'd never seen Teresa this excited so I was immediately pumped with positive energy. I gave everyone a pleasant nod and wave.

"Juan this is our lawyer, Bailey, and our A&R, Cindy, from Elite Records. Ladies, this is the new addition to Last Horizon, Juan," Teresa announced.

Everyone in the room started clapping and stood to their feet. I was over whelmed and begin to tear up. I was speechless. Even Matt looked happy. "Thank you, thank you, thank you," I said looking around the room.

Bailey pulled out a contract and a gold pen and placed it in front of me. She went through the sixteen-page document, quickly explaining each clause and told me to initial every page. To be honest I really wasn't paying attention to anything she said. I was just happy to sign that contract.

Every time I initialed my name I was counting money and getting closer to a better relationship with my father. On the very last page, I saw that the other three guys and Teresa already signed. Though I knew way better than to sign a contract before reading it, I didn't want this to stand between me and my dreams. So I signed and it felt great. I felt the power of success with every stroke of that pen.

Cindy then explained to everyone that I had to begin working on the next album by next week. She said Elite Records needed for this album to be completed and turned in by mid-March in order for us to have the album out for the summer. This meant that we would have to begin promoting a new single around that time as well.

Teresa then explained to everyone that we had to begin doing press by that weekend. She also explained that since the group has a new member, we have to tell that to the fans. That meant we had to do interviews with radio, television, and magazines right away.

My excitement turned into worry because I didn't know if the group's fans would accept me. They were used to seeing and hearing Leo. I hoped I had what it takes to live up to Leo and to exceed what he did. I expressed this concern during the meeting.

Bailey explained that the media loves drama and this would make the group more appealing. "People are going to want to know what happened to Leo in the group. Was he kicked out, did he leave, and why? Allow the older members in the group to handle those questions. You should never comment on that situation because it could taint your imagine," she said to me.

Teresa added, "Even though we all know that Leo was kicked out of the group for his drug issues, we're going to say he decided to leave because he wanted to go solo." The other guys nodded in agreement.

I'm still confused about what happened to Leo. That just didn't sound right to me. But hey, it was my time and I was ready to do what I had to do.

During the meeting we were prepped on what to say to the media. Some of the things were flat out lies but I guessed that is what celebrities had to do to keep parts of their lives private. Like firstly, they told me to tell the press my age was 18. I do understand that they were trying to appeal to a young audience, and if this was what I had to do then, oh well. I knew people that actually know me will be confused but hopefully they would understand. I learned then that the other group members were actually in their mid to late 20's, but all were listed under the age of 21. It made me wonder what else was a lie.

Because I was so excited and didn't want to rain on my own parade I allowed myself to stay in the dark about things. Even when I really knew the truth I would ignore it, and pretend not to know. I was then told that Cal was actually Teresa's son but I could never talk about it to anyone, probably because people would wonder why he's even in the group in the first place. At least that's what I wondered during rehearsals. He was the oldest and didn't really contribute anything to the group. But outside of the group, I would admit he was the coolest to be around. He seemed to be more easy-going.

After the meeting, Teresa and the guys gave me a tour of the house. In the basement of the house there is a full rehearsal hall, gym, and recording studio. She explained to me that the group lived there and that I would have to move in soon. Growing up, I lived in a trailer that barely had running water so living in this big beautiful estate seemed like heaven to me. I just made a "come up" and wasn't planning on going back to scraps.

"Do you have a girlfriend," Teresa asked.

"Yes, I do," I replied.

"Well to be honest you're going to have to end that relationship," she said.

"Really? Why? We've been together for about two years," I argued.

Teresa went on to explain to me how my life as I knew it as was about to change overnight. She said that family and friends would not understand so it's best to cut them off and not allow them into this part of my life. "I will pick you a very nice girl that understands this lifestyle, a girl who has her own money," she said.

I've never been the materialistic, superficial type of person so I still didn't understand what the point of cutting off all my friends and family was. I thought they were the ones that deserved to see me at my best. They needed to know that I didn't allow fame or money to change me. If that was what this side of life was about, I didn't like it. Still, if I wanted to be a part of it I had to surrender. I never thought I would have to choose my dreams over my friends and family. This part of the deal really haunted me because one of the main reasons why I wanted to do this was so that my family could enjoy the good life.

"So you guys need to be rehearsing every day this week at least eight hours a day," Teresa announced to all of us.

"I have school and work this week; can we schedule a time so there's no conflict for me?" I quickly asked.

"Juan, I'm sorry but this is the business. You guys have to rehearse every day from eight a.m. to four p.m. I'm going to need for you guys' routines to be tight. I need to see flawless performances.

"I'm sorry you have school and all but to be honest, you're about to make way more money now than you would with any degree. How do you think we live like this?

"As far as your job, you can quit that right away, we'll pay you two hundred dollars weekly until you guys start doing shows again. We're going to need you to move in here anyways, so no need to worry about paying rent; I'll give you the money to break your lease.

"Also as far as school, you're not going to be able to do school and be on tour. I already have you guys booked on a Japanese Tour that starts in Tokyo this summer," she said.

I just nodded to agree. This was a lot to take in at once. Teresa could sell water to a whale, and I must have been Moby Dick because she got me *sold*.

Though I would have liked to live this type of lifestyle, I was nervous about it. Maybe all this was just happening way too fast for me. Just a week ago my life was regular, and now all of a sudden it changed.

Quitting my job at the print shop and breaking my lease would be the easiest tasks. I only had about a year left in college before I receive my degree. I would be a fool to drop out now, but then again, not really, especially when upgrading to this type of life. My mom wouldn't like this one bit. David…. Oh, wow, David would be crushed. Even if we decided to stay together it would be nearly impossible for us to see each other because of my work schedule with Last Horizon. I had a lot in front of me to do and little time to do all these life-changing things just to align myself for this opportunity. None of it was going to be easy but if I really wanted this, it had to be done.

Sacrificing everything in my life just for my dream drained me emotionally, physically, spiritually and mentally. I hoped it was going to be worth it. All of a sudden I wasn't excited anymore. I felt like I was getting what I wanted and the price was my life and soul. Was this how the devil presents himself? I thought if this was to ever happen to me I would recognize it, but I didn't feel like I was making the wrong or right decision. I just felt like this was how it had to be.

TRACK 6:
When Doves Cry

The ride home that night was a quiet one. I turned off my radio and just listened to my tires glide across the highway pavement. Thinking of all the things I had to do to align myself with this opportunity made me feel like a zombie. I didn't feel like I was living. I was losing my soul. I had become so numb to everything around me. I called David before I got home and told him to meet me at my apartment later that night. I already told him that we had to talk and it was serious. By the tone in his voice I could tell he was already expecting the worst.

So many thoughts were running through my head. I didn't know how I would build up the nerve to tell David we can't possibly be together— especially after I told him this situation wouldn't change anything about our relationship.

When David arrived at my apartment that night I wasn't nervous. I just felt like I had to do this. I began to look at him as if he was my enemy and was trying to hold me back from my dreams, though deep down I knew that wasn't the truth. I just had to find a way for me to get through it. Making him my enemy was the only way I could do it.

"We can't be together," I said as he closed the door to my apartment. I just wanted to get it out quickly and be done with it.

"I figured this was about to happen. Juan, I love you. Everything I do in my life is for us. I don't understand how you could just throw us away. I should be your dream. You're my dream", David cried.

"It's a complicated situation that I don't think will work for both of us. We're never going to see each other anymore, David. I'm dropping out of school next week", I said boldly.

"What?! Are you stupid?! Do they have some type of spell on you?! You're losing your mind for this dream! And I'm not going to stand around and watch you throw your life away for 'YOUR DREAM.' Goodbye, Juan," he said with tears in his eyes as he turned to open the door and walk out.

I quickly grabbed his arm to pull him back in.

"Don't you turn your back, and walk away from me", I said harshly.

I felt myself watching myself from across the room. I had never spoken to David in that tone. He slapped me so hard that my ears ranged. I immediately grabbed him and threw him to the wall that's perpendicular to the door, hitting his head on the thermostat. The metal casing from the thermostat fell to the floor making a loud crashing sound which brought me back into my body. We both stood there for a few seconds looking at each other as we both began to breathe hard. David looked at me hopelessly and defeated. I stared him down like I was going to kill him. He grabbed the door knob and walked out quickly without saying a word.

I felt evil watching David leave like that. I felt heartless but I also felt this was the only way. I stayed up the whole night contemplating calling David to apologize and just be done with the group. But I was already moving forward and I didn't want to take any steps backward.

The very next day I went down to my school to un-enroll myself. The hardest part was to leave David, and since that was done everything else should be easy. I was so emotionally numb that it didn't faze me much to leave. I just kept going with the flow. I didn't care what others may think or say about me dropping out because they would soon come to understand.

During the rest of that week I was over Teresa's house rehearsing and recording with the group. By the end of each day I was so exhausted that I didn't feel like driving all the way back to College Park so I would stay the night there. I began to see why I had to drop out of school and why I had to move into the home with the rest of the group.

That weekend we started to do press interviews. We went out to the Bi-Annual Hair Show in Atlanta to do a small performance, sign autographs, and to announce the obvious changes within the group. Since this would be my first public performance with the group, I was extremely nervous. We only had to perform one song, which was the group's biggest single that won them their awards, "Young and in Love".

As we were introduced, I was transformed from the nervous guy to the overconfident sex symbol. From the first moment on stage, I could tell that the crowd loved me. I'm not sure that they even realized I wasn't Leo. Or maybe they were familiar with the song. Either way, they all were swaying and singing along. I see Marcel in the audience and he's singing along like everyone else. He noticed that I saw him and gave me the thumbs up. I gave him a wink to let him know I recognized his presence. I hadn't heard from Marcel since the night I was at his house.

After the performance the crowd went wild for Last Horizon. Their loud screams and applause gave me a high that I wanted so much more of. The other three guys all congratulated me on a job well done. That meant a lot to me because I felt like their future was in my hands. They trusted me to carry them to the next level.

We were then set up at a booth to sign autographs. During this time I was able to feel like a star. I felt like people really cared about who I was, until a fan asked what happened to Leo. I just pretended to not hear her because I was instructed to not answer those types of questions. As I'm looking down signing an autograph I heard, "You can make that out to Marcel."

I looked up to see Marcel standing there waiting for my autograph. I got really nervous because I wasn't sure how to feel. After I signed he said, "Thanks" and walked away.

I'm glad he didn't try to hold a conversation because I didn't want the other guys in the group to get suspicious about anything, even though they had nothing to be suspicious about. I think my own insecurity about my sexuality had my mind thinking things that weren't apparent.

After the autographs, we were guided to speak with lots of press and media organizations. Now we were about to break the news about the changes in the group. Everything will then be public and I really needed to make sure I was on point every time I hit the stage.

Later that evening I received a text from Marcel saying, "Thanks for the autograph, superstar." I immediately called him to thank him. From there we began to talk about everything that was happening at that moment in my life. I even told him that the "girlfriend" I had was actually a guy and his name was David.

Talking to Marcel about everything that was happening made me feel relieved. I felt like he understood how I felt about my dreams. From there, we constantly talked and texted whenever I had free time. Because I had become so busy with the group, we could never find time to hang out. But I now considered him to be a good friend. He knew things about me that no one else knew and was like me in so many ways.

TRACK 7:
What's Goin' On

In the following weeks the split between the group and Leo was buzzing throughout the industry. Almost every urban magazine was talking about it. Some said he was kicked out the group and others said he left the group. Leo even went to some other magazines to tell his side of the story. He said he left the group because the manager was stealing his money. He said he did 95% of the recording for the group and didn't receive anything for it. He also said a lot of bad things about the group members I didn't agree with because they seemed to be great to me, at least at that time. He mentioned that Cal was Teresa's son and that's the only reason he's in the group because he has no talent. He said that Kev was extremely jealous of him because he got all the shine from the fans. And Matt was the only person he actually trusted in the group because they were friends before they were in the group together. And he explained that they lived a mafia type of lifestyle that he refused to elaborate on.

When what Leo said reached the ears of Teresa and the guys they immediately went on defensive about it. Though they already admitted to me that Cal was indeed Teresa's son, they then added that he used to be a great singer years ago. They explained Cal's vocal cords were ruined in a car accident. He must have swallowed windshield glass because I couldn't see what a car accident had to do with his vocal cords, but okay. I just took their word for it.

Kev said the jealously was the other way around. I was told not to believe what Leo was putting out in the media because he was mad he was kicked out of the group. Knowing there is always more than one side to a story, I decided to block out those accusations that Leo made about the group and management. At this point I didn't care. I just wanted to move on and get out there in front of the world.

The more time I spent with these guys, the more we became like family. They were truly like brothers to me. Even Matt and I were talking like we'd known each other for years. He and Leo were close and he didn't care to see anyone replace him. That's why he treated me distantly in the beginning. I could definitely understand that.

Outside of the group setting, he gave me good advice about performing and warned me about things to look out for, when it comes to Teresa, like her ability to turn on people quickly. Ironically, I had grown closer to Matt than the other two guys.

Time began to move along so quickly. It was already the beginning of March and Elite Records was asking about the group's second album. They wanted us to fly out to Los Angeles to present it to them. This would be their first time seeing me face to face. They want to capitalize on the drama with Leo being out of the group while it's still fresh in people's minds. We've worked every day on this album and I personally feel like it tops the group's first album.

Despite the drama and media blitz, I know I've worked hard on this project. Though I think the record company is smart about its timing. It seems like people buy into the gimmick rather than the quality of the music. Honestly, in my opinion, Last Horizon was a gimmick in the first place. Having four extremely attractive guys singing and dancing to catchy music is good enough to sell a million records to screaming teenagers.

When we got into our meeting with Elite Records we performed all the songs from our new album. The record executives seemed to like it. After the last song, the CEO looks at Teresa and said, "It's a good album but they don't have a comeback single."

He told us that he would set up a studio session for us in LA to work with "SupaBass", which was the hottest producer out at the time, with three Top Ten Singles on the radio. I was already humbled to be working with the record company but to work with SupaBass would take us directly to the top.

While we were in LA I received a voicemail from David, telling me he really wanted to speak to me. From the sound of his voice, I can tell that it was something important. Even though I was feeling like I was moving on with my life I couldn't deny that David was still important to me. I still considered him to be a really good friend. I knew that I couldn't call him back while I was around anyone in the group because I didn't want them in my personal business.

After our long day in LA we went back to our hotel. Once everyone was asleep I went down to the hotel lobby to call David. I could tell from his voice that he had been drinking which was so not like David. I'd seen him drink maybe three times since I'd known him and definitely not as much as he sounded like he had.

He told me how much he was missing me and wanting to at least keep an open communication between us, even though we were not together. Being very concerned about David I agreed to communicate with him on a regular basis. I told him I would text him when I got back to Atlanta so we can possibly meet up for lunch. He seemed to be excited about that idea and so was I. I had really missed him too.

A few days later we were in one of LA's finest studios recording with Grammy-winning producer SupaBass. The group's chemistry with SupaBass was so great that we ended up recording way more than was expected. Even though most of the time it was just me and SupaBass in the studio all day and night. The other guys in the group and Teresa were out somewhere in LA partying so hard that each day they woke up with hangovers. I was beginning to feel like I was carrying this group on my own. I actually felt like I was recording my debut solo album, since I was always in the studio alone. Though having the opportunity to work with SupaBass felt to be worth it because he made me feel very comfortable while recording. He was a fan of the group and was excited to work with us. He also helped me build my confidence as the new lead singer.

One of the songs we recorded was called "My Turn", which spoke about someone who has been constantly trying to succeed but has failed over and over again. But now it's their turn to succeed. I related so much to this song. It was by far one of my favorite songs I recorded for this album. Over the course of three days we were able to complete five songs with SupaBass. This was good because now the record label would have so much to choose from.

While working in the studio with SupaBass, Fred-T would stop by to listen in. Fred-T used to be part of the boy group Heart Break 3 better known as HB3. I used to listen to their music when I was in high school. I remembered all the girls going crazy over those guys. They broke up a couple of years ago.

Even though Fred-T wasn't a lead singer in the group, he was now working on his first solo project. He was actually planning to use one of the songs that I wrote for Last Horizon on his album. Fred-T had a lot of media attention at the time because he had admitted to being molested by his group's manager. I could only imagine the crazy things he'd been through working in the music industry. For a little while Fred-T and I kept in contact via text and internet.

When Teresa found out that we were actually friends she forced me to stop talking to him and demanded that I delete his number. She said that she didn't want me to be affiliated with Fred-T. I never totally understood why though.

Within days we were all back in Elite Records office and they were excited about the music we recorded with SupaBass. They were so excited, that they decided to keep all five songs for the album. Because of the five newly added songs to the album they decided to scrap five songs that were produced by Maestro. But that wasn't much since Maestro had produced over 90% of the album anyways. They titled this album "Second Introduction", which was the title of one of the songs we recorded with SupaBass.

The first single from this album would be "How Do You Like Me Now", which talked about leaving your old relationship and getting with someone new that's an upgrade from your previous relationship. This song was a definite hit and extremely controversial for the group since I replaced Leo. I loved the song but I didn't want to appear to be too cocky since this would be my first introduction to the music industry.

TRACK 8:
How Do You Like Me Now?

When we returned to Atlanta we began working on photo shoots, choreography, and treatments for the music video to "How Do You Like Me Now". In the midst of being so busy, I was able to keep an open communication between me and David. He seemed to be doing better. I was even able to communicate with Marcel. I actually planned to take the two of them out for lunch after we finished shooting the music video.

The morning before for the video shoot was a disaster. Teresa had fired Cal from the group because he came in extremely late the night before. He was completely hung over, but this was nothing new to me. Kev, Matt, and I begged and pleaded with Teresa to allow him back into the group. Cal being Teresa's son, you would think he would care a bit more, but that wasn't the case.

Cal was a good person but extremely spoiled. He would throw tantrums and fits with Teresa regularly; you would think he was the lead singer. He had a very childish mentally as if he could do what he wanted and get bailed out if he messed up. I heard Teresa make up hundreds of excuses for his behavior. She had threatened to put him out of the group and her house three times since I'd been around. I could only imagine that this had been going on forever. We told her that we will watch over him and make sure he stopped drinking.

Because Cal's eyes were so red and puffy, he had to wear sunglasses for the video shoot. I could smell the liquor rising from his pores. He didn't seem like himself at all, I just figured it was because he was hung over.

Because of this altercation we were an hour late for our own video shoot. Arriving at a video studio in Decatur to see all the camera crew, fans, extras, and huge backdrops with our name on it felt great. This moment was another moment I'd dreamed about. Since we were late, the director wanted to get the choreographed dance shots first.

We took our places dressed in all black on an all white set with our name in the background. During about the fourth take the director yelled "Cut." He told Cal to stay in sync with the rest of us. I was instantly embarrassed for him because there were lots of extras and fans watching. As the play back rolled, I heard a hard thump behind me and people began to scream. I turned around to see Cal laid out on the ground. Matt and Kev rushed to his side while I stood there in a daze because I had no idea what was going on.

"Call an ambulance," Teresa yelled as she rushed to his side. The director yelled for his crew, extra, and fans to all move back.

It took about ten minutes for the ambulance to arrive. The paramedics put Cal on the stretcher and I saw he was breathing. They rushed him into the ambulance. A sense of sadness went through everyone. Even the director was extremely concerned.

After the ambulance pulled away Teresa turned to us and the director and told us to continue shooting. She said she will head to the hospital and come back to the shoot later.

Since Cal was not going to be there for the remainder of the shoot, we would have to shoot our solo scenes. They would have to use whatever they have already of the dance sequence in the final edit of the music video. Doing the rest of the shoot was so empty without Cal. Not knowing what was wrong with him bothered the three of us. They assured me that he had done forty-five minute shows while being hung over in the past so he should be fine. After about thirteen hours we were done shooting the video. Though I was excited, I was saddened because we were still unsure what was going on with Cal. We called Teresa, and she instructed us to come to the hospital right away.

When we arrived to the hospital I could tell by the look on Teresa's face that she had been crying all day. "Cal had a light stroke," she said sadly.

My heart fell to floor. I didn't even know what a "light stroke" was but it didn't sound good. It sounded like something that only happens to older people. She said the doctors are not sure what caused it but they have run all the tests they could, and he should be home in about a week. The doctor suggested Cal take it easy for the next few months, which is perfectly bad timing for Last Horizon. Teresa planned for us to continue to promote the single and video but we wouldn't do any public appearances without Cal.

She demanded we deny this incident ever happened, especially if it came up in the media. If these types of situations went public, the record label would pull all funding from the group and we would be left with no deal. At that moment I felt a change in Matt and Kev. They both grabbed and hugged me tight.

"You ready," Matt asked.

"I think so, I have no choice," I replied.

Since Cal was in the hospital and we weren't going to be making any public appearances, I decided to use this time to hang out with David and Marcel. I invited them both out for lunch at the sports bar in Atlantic Station. Teresa still kept close tabs on our whereabouts and even gave us a curfew now since Cal's incident. Though I understood her tactics as a manager, I didn't agree with them. But I abided by her rules to stay out of trouble with her.

When we all finally arrived at the sports bar, I felt good being able to see David. I'd been working so hard with the group and seeing him felt refreshing. Though I would admit that having Marcel and David there at one time was a bit awkward because of what happened between Marcel and me. I wondered how Marcel felt because he knew of my and David's relationship. I would never tell David, even if we became strictly just friends someday.

After the sports bar we all sat in the Atlantic Station parking garage and talked for what seemed like forever. I had laughed again, and it came from a good place, not because I was trying to fit into the group.

Marcel ended up leaving first, so David and I remained there talking. During this conversation we both agreed to allow each other to move on. We also promised to support each other, no matter what. This made me feel like a million bucks. To have his support made me want to work harder on the music because he understood my aspirations. He wasn't the messy type of guy to put me on blast in the media, and I was grateful for that.

Right before we parted ways we gave each other a hug that led to a long-awaited passionate kiss. This kiss felt like a million kisses all in one. I could tell he missed me and I knew he could tell that I've missed him. I felt a tear from his eyes drop to my cheeks.

TRACK 9:
Welcome to the Jungle

A few days later, Cal returned home from the hospital and we were all so happy. He seemed to be ready to jump back into the swing of things. Even though the doctor told him to take it easy, his excitement about being back gave us strength. Since our video was set to premiere in a few days we began to do promo. The video came out great and with the tricks of editing, it was hard to tell that Cal was missing from most of the shots.

We were scheduled to fly to New York to premiere the video on New Beat. New Beat was a popular music video countdown television show that came on All Stars TV, better known as ASTV. Most current major recording artist was brought to the show to perform or to do interviews. This appearance meant the world to the success of the group because it was the group's reintroduction, the introduction to me and our new sound. I was extremely nervous because this could make or break us.

Flying out to New York was great, being that it was my first time in the Big Apple. It was amazing to see all the buildings and the lights in Times Square. It all looked as it does on TV.

While there, we had a press conference, where many media outlets came out to interview us about the group's comeback. They would be asking questions about the new album, which would come out May 24th. And of course they would ask about the drama that led to Leo's separation from the group.

It honestly seemed as if many people were more concerned about the drama with Leo, than they were with our new music. I didn't really mind because I knew all of this attention will lead to record sells somehow.

When we arrived to do New Beat, it felt so surreal. I had watched this show since high school. The set looked a bit smaller in person than it did on TV. The fans there loved us and the video.

This was the first TV appearance we made as a group. The social media and fans response to me was all so over whelming. Though there were some hardcore fans of Leo, they still seemed to just love the group as a whole and accepted me.

The video for "How Do You Like Me Now" later became #1 for an entire month and lasted on the countdown well into July.

Because of the popularity of "How Do You Like Me Now", we were asked to return to New Beat to perform live. Performing live on New Beat, I knew, was my opportunity to be what the fans expected me to be. Even though they heard the new single, hearing me live could make a world of a difference. And it went so great that we began getting offers to perform on many major daytime, primetime, news shows, and even a national summer tour. I then realized Teresa hadn't mentioned anything else about that Japanese Tour in months. We hadn't even applied for passports or VISAs. I wondered if there was ever even an actual tour or if she made that all up.

By this time it was mid-May, just a week away from Last Horizon's second album release. We were so busy and tired from rehearsing, doing TV shows, and interviews. We had been all over the country promoting the new album. There were huge billboards, posters, and radio and TV commercials everywhere announcing this album. Elite Records really gave us a big budget for this project.

Even though our budget was big, my bank account barely had two hundred and fifty dollars in it at one time. And the two hundred that I was promised in the beginning was somehow reduced down to a hundred a week. Later the hundred dollars was reduced to fifty, soon after I was getting absolutely nothing. So my student loans, credit cards, car note, etc. was barely paid. I would have to call home to my Mom and ask her to pay some of my bills for me.

They already sent over our budget and treatment for the next music video and single, "She Got It" which was also produced by SupaBass. This song was going to be our summer hit. It was an up-tempo tune that spoke about a girl that is everything; no matter her size, complexion, or height, she got it all. Though this was not my favorite song on the album I knew that we could promote "good self-esteem" to our fans and supporters. Those types of songs seemed to hit an emotional nerve with people.

Since we were doing so much business in New York, it was decided to shoot the video there as well. The setting for this video was Times Square. I got that natural high feeling again being at the heart of New York's most popular spot shooting my second music video. The lights from the billboards and advertisements warmed my spirit. It was like seeing Christmas lights and decorations as a child. So many people walked by just to watch; it felt amazing. I felt like I was a movie star and I mattered. The video shoot went really well compared to the first one. No one was hung over, and no one was rushed to the hospital.

Days after the video shoot was our album release date. This was another day I had seriously dreamed of my entire life. My first and the group's second album was hitting the stores. This 13-song masterpiece would be the beginning of so many more albums to come. I had received text and calls from everyone including my father congratulating me. This was exactly what I had hoped for.

Later that night, the record company set up an album release party for us at a popular night club in Manhattan. There we had a red carpet and so many celebrities showed up to show their love and respect for the group. Even Michael G. showed up. Michael G. is a music mogul that ran the extremely successful record label, Hit Maker Records. All the artists he'd signed went Platinum and beyond. I'd always wanted to work with Michael G., even though he had his share of drama in the media. Working with Michael G. meant you were of importance. Lots of the most iconic stars in the business worked with Michael G. I learned then that he and Teresa were good friends, and they actually had known each other for many years.

He walked over to us and gave all the guys hugs and when he got to me he said "Congratulations, you've made a great album. And welcome to my world, my industry."

Though he smiled, his energy felt strange to me. I almost felt like he possessed me for a second. I had to quickly pat myself down; it seemed as if he stole something from me.

Just days after the album release we were back on the road now promoting not only the album but our newest single "She Got It". The work seemed to never end. I swear I was only living on maybe three to four hours of sleep a day.

Later that June, we started the summer Hot Jamz Tour along with other major acts. During the beginning of the Hot Jamz tour it felt amazing to see the fans in each city. The group seemed to be getting along well and management seemed to be pleased with the work we were doing.

We were also preparing to perform at the ASTV Award show which would be in July. We found out that we were nominated for two awards, "Best Song" and "Best Group or Duo". Even though we were two short of the amount of nominations the group had last year, it was still good. At least it felt good to me.

When it was finally the day of the ASTV Awards I was feeling great. Nothing could bring me down that day. Out of nowhere, I received a text from Marcel saying, "I just want to die, I don't know what to do." Immediately I text him back and I asked him, "what's wrong?" My heart began to pound and I wasn't sure what to think. While waiting for him to text me back, I knew that I couldn't worry about him right now. I had so much to do and I needed my energy to be on point. This performance had to be perfect.

TRACK 10:
Waterfalls

When we arrived at the ASTV Awards, we walked the red carpet doing interviews and taking hundreds of pictures. During our interviews the media was still asking about Leo. When we looked around, Leo was also walking the red carpet and talking to media as well. This was my first time ever seeing him in person. Teresa told us to just continue on like we didn't see him, but for some reason I couldn't help but look back. Looking back I finally gained eye contact with Leo.

Even though he was many feet away I can tell he saw us too. Cal and Kev made jokes about walking back there to beat him up for the things he said about them in the media. I really didn't care as much because I didn't know him, and without him leaving Last Horizon I wouldn't be there; I actually owed him a "Thank You".

During the award show we were back stage just about to perform. We said our group prayer and the music intro played, signaling us to get into place. It seemed like every moment got me higher and higher. During this performance, I took the time to look at all the faces in the audience as I sang "How Do You Like Me Now". I didn't want this moment to slide away so fast. I tried to live in it as much as I could. After the performance, the crowd gave us a standing ovation.

Looking at all these celebrities and people I'd admired standing up for me took me even higher. Even Leo stood up. He probably stood up because he didn't want to get caught on camera sitting down looking shady. Directly after the performance the nominations for "Best Group or Duo" were being presented.

"Amongst so much competition, the Best Group or Duo Award goes to..... Last Horizon," the presenter shouts. My body was filled with chills; I felt light headed. We ran back on stage to receive our award and thanked God and everyone involved. While we're saying our "thank yous", I could see Leo making his way to the stage. My heart began to pound because this could turn out really bad.

When he reached the stage the audience erupted. Some are cheering and some are booing. Leo grabbed the microphone and said, "You guys forgot to thank me for making you who you are..."

The microphone was then cut off and we were escorted off, leaving Leo standing there. Security guards rushed the stage to escort Leo out. It was so crazy. Now of course the media would want to know how we felt about Leo interrupting our acceptance speech. Kev and Cal both were furious. They wanted to hurt him bad. Matt seemed to not be phased at all as if he knew Leo was going to do that. Teresa actually found what Leo did quite amusing. Though she laughed, she assured us that Leo will be dealt with and we wouldn't have to worry about him anymore.

Later that night, after the award show and after parties, we all went back to the hotel. (Whenever we stayed at hotels we would get three rooms. Cal and I would share, Matt and Kev shared, and Teresa would have a room to herself.) Even though my day was filled with excitement and craziness, Marcel was still on my mind. So I called him immediately.

After trying to call him several times, he didn't answer and I realized he never replied to my text earlier that day. I began to get extremely worried about him, then my phone rang and it was him. When I answered the phone, I can tell he was crying due to the trembles in his voice. I could barely hear what he was saying. Then I heard him say "HIV". My heart hit the floor and my mouth literally dropped. After calming down a bit, he explained that he just found out he was HIV positive. I began to pray for him on the phone. He said that he wanted to kill himself and even though I tried to talk him out of it, I can't imagine how he felt getting this news. All I can tell him is, "Please hang in there." I told him I will be there to see him when I return to Atlanta. I felt helpless as a friend now. I didn't know what to say in this situation. All I could do was pray for him.

The next day we flew back to Atlanta and all I could think about was Marcel. I contacted him as soon as the plane landed. Since we didn't have anything scheduled for the next couple days, I decided to go spend time with him. I was able to tag along on one of his doctor visits. Seeing him go through this process really made me emotional and I just wanted to be there for him even more. Though I thought that Marcel would be more careful since he worked at a clinic, I still felt bad for him. He said he hadn't told his family and didn't think he ever would. He assured me that I'm the only person outside of the doctors and nurses at the clinic that knew. I realized that I meant more to Marcel than I thought. He really trusted me as a friend. He said he knew who could have given it to him and he was going to contact them soon.

Seeing him go through this was sad. I've definitely heard of people getting HIV, but I had never known one personally. He didn't look like HIV, he still looked the same. I guess it's true that you can't tell someone's status by looking at them. Staying protected has to be a priority. To lift his spirits I cooked dinner for him and spent the entire day with him. Even though Teresa was calling me constantly to see where I was, I kept telling her I was on my way but there was an accident on Highway 400 and it will take hours before I'll be back. I'm sure she could probably see through my lies but I didn't care. I felt like Marcel needed someone by his side at that time, so I didn't leave his house until about eight that night. It was my duty to be a friend and I was down for the cause, even if it meant I'd have to face Teresa.

TRACK 11:
We Need
A Resolution

When I got back to Teresa's house that night she called an emergency group meeting as soon as I walked in the door. She was obviously upset because I had been gone all day. I told her that I was under the impression that this was a day off for us. She told me that we don't get days off.

"You are my national recording artist that lives in my house. I make the rules and you will do as I say," she said.

"Don't forget we can replace you", Kev chimed in. I turned and looked quickly at Kev. I'm immediately confused because Kev is now talking down to me as if he's paying me personally. Kev was acting like he's the manager and I'm just a "bag boy". Cal and Matt never made eye contact with me. They both just looked off into space, not saying a word. I felt betrayed by Kev. He was usually cool and easy to talk to, but all of a sudden he'd turned against me. I started to think he was either on drugs or bi-polar. He was notorious for changing his mind suddenly for no apparent reason. Kev was the type of guy that would agree with you privately but get in front of others and disagree. The other guys and I would call him "Flip Flop" at times because of it. I was starting to see what Leo may have spoken about to the media.

I will admit, since the release of our album I had been a lot more relaxed and opinionated because I felt like they really needed me more at this point. Kicking me out the group would not be wise because that will cause the record company to lose faith in the group all together. So I knew I could have more freedom because they can't erase my face off the album covers.

Teresa constantly reminded us that any one of us could be replaced, just as Leo was. Out of fear of being put out of the group we all just did what she wanted us to do. We all were living under her roof; even though it was a beautiful home I missed my freedom. Being able to just go to Wal-Mart was something I longed for. It wasn't even about causing pandemonium, but because Teresa wanted that control over all of us. If I was on the phone talking to anyone, she would always ask who I was talking to and why. This situation seemed to be so good on the outside but it began to feel like a prison. Though we had begun making a little money from doing the Hot Jamz tour, we owed Teresa 20% as our manager, plus a newly additional 40% for "living in her home." I thought when I had an album out I would be able to go buy a house or even a car. Instead we were living in a huge fancy house, and driving fancy cars which were all owned by Teresa.

After the meeting I went to my room to think. I began to question everything about this situation. Why was Kev so upset if today was our off day? Why aren't we making any money? How can Teresa afford to live in this house? How was she affording her cars and lifestyle? I understand the group had a very successful year last year and maybe that's how she was able to afford everything. But why is she charging us 40% on top of her contractual 20%? We are her project that's an expense that she has to swallow. And why do I have a curfew if I'm paying rent? Hell, why do I have a curfew and I'm over the age of eighteen in REAL life?

So many questions were flowing through my head when a soft quiet knock hit my room door. "Come in," I said.

It was Matt and he wanted to talk. He told me to be careful in this situation and watch everything around me. I asked him for specifics but he assured me that everything will make sense really soon. "Don't expect to get rich doing this. There are so many things going on around you that you don't realize. Keep your eyes open," he said.

I asked him to tell me everything but I knew he wasn't going to do it. I can tell what he said was sincere and from a good place. He told me to make the best of this situation for myself. Being so confused about what he was telling me I began to feel like this whole thing could have been a huge mistake. When he left my room I began to ponder everything that was going on. I didn't sleep at all that night.

Even though the next day was supposed to be another off day, Teresa made it an all-day rehearsal for us. She demanded that we rehearse since we were continuing the Hot Jamz tour the next day in Huntsville, Alabama. Throughout the entire rehearsal I just went through the motions. Kev stopped rehearsal several times to comment on my vocals, saying I was off key and my dance steps were off. Even though I was really angry and I knew he was probably just picking on me, I didn't have much to say back. I just allowed him to pick. Even though he wasn't a singer or even a great dancer, I'd let him feel good about himself. I'd allow him to feel this sense of artificial power. I never wanted to conflict with the guys in the group because I truly did admire all of their hard work even though they only lip-synced. Plus these were my brothers; I didn't want to fight them when I had the whole world to fight against.

Kev complained the entire rehearsal; he even began to say how much better Leo was than me. It hurt a lot to hear him say those things but I pretended to not care much. I can tell he may have wanted me to quit the group. His antics weren't working, because my dreams were so much bigger than Last Horizon.

The next day right before we went out on stage in Huntsville, Kev came to me and whispered in my ear "I'm sorry man."

I quickly gave him a pat on the back and said, "It's alright, man, we in this together." I felt like I just rolled the dice and began to play the game. I didn't mean anything I just said to Kev. I really wanted him to fall off stage and break his neck. But I knew that I couldn't allow this energy to distract me from doing a good performance. For the first time since I'd been with the group I felt like my heart wasn't there. I felt confused and empty. Kev really rubbed me the wrong way and it would be hard for me to be cool with him again. If I was to overcome this situation I would definitely fake it until I made it.

It was normally Kev's thing to take off his shirt during the show but I felt like being a "bad ass", so I took off my shirt.

"What in the hell are you doing", Kev yelled to me.

Thankfully the rest of their microphones were turned off because the fans would have heard him. I pretended to not hear him and proceeded to even throw my shirt into the audience. The fans were going wild. When it came to the part when Kev was supposed to take off his shirt, no one really seemed to care. They gave him some cheers and applause but definitely not like other shows.

"Faggot ass bitch," Kev yells to me as we exit the stage.

I know he's talking to me but I'm great at ignoring people. I just pretended to not hear him at all. Cal grabbed Kev and told him to calm down but Kev pushed Cal back. Cal got pissed and began to tussle with Kev.

"I'm just trying to help you dude," Cal kept repeating. A security guard broke the two of them up.

"Good Job," Matt told me with a wink.

"What's going on," Teresa screamed as she came to stand between us all.

"This fuckin' faggot takes off his shirt, knowing damn well that that's my job," Kev yelled.

"Kev, you guys had a great show please calm down," Teresa said.

The whole time I stood there with a little smart-ass smirk on my face. I knew Kev's only talent is his body. Though I knew what I did wasn't in good intent, I knew it would piss him off, so I did it. I also knew this would really establish bad vibes between Kev and me but I didn't care. Why should I when he didn't care about the way he flipped out on me the other day? Teresa told me to never do that again and I agreed that I wouldn't.

From that day I had begun to notice the separation within Last Horizon. I noticed how Matt and Cal didn't talk to Kev so much. Though that was their normal behavior, it was all coming clear to me. Kev seemed to always want to take control, even though we were all equal in the group. Teresa allowed him to take on the leadership role even though she knew the tension it brought to the group. I seriously had begun to think he had a mental problem or maybe just some insecurity issues. I decided to play it cool with him for the sake of the group, but I wouldn't

allow him near my personal life.

TRACK 12:
Love You Forever

For the rest of the tour I kept an obvious distance from Kev, even though when we did interviews or photo shoots it appeared that we were all getting along just fine. I'd changed so much since my first day in the group. I use to be so caring and compassionate to everyone, but now I saw myself being and thinking just as dirty as the rest of the people in this industry.

Though I didn't like the person I was becoming, I knew I had to build tough skin if I was going to make it in this business. I began to learn how to turn it on and off. I was great and humble with the fans but when it came to personal time with the group I was very withdrawn and distant. I just did what was required and that was it. Whenever we would have time to ourselves, I would go off on my own. Matt and I would spend time talking occasionally.

I didn't have much of an issue with Cal, but since Teresa was his mom I didn't feel safe talking with him about certain things regarding my feelings towards the group. Whenever he would get upset with his mom about personal issues, he spoke out of turn about some of their family secrets. The things he would say were so hard to believe since he was mad at the time.

On the last show we did in July, Teresa came down on us hard about our performance. She said there were lots of missed steps in the choreography especially from Cal. She accused him of being hung over and drunk during the performance so she threatened to put him out of the group for the millionth time. She also threatened to not pay him for the show. In a heat of rage Cal threw a laptop through the tour bus window. There was glass everywhere. The tour security guards came on to the bus to hold Cal down.

Teresa would argue and scream along with him whenever they had a disagreement. There was no resolution to the issue when they got into confrontations with each other. You couldn't tell they were actually mother and son when they feuded. They both would say some of the cruelest things to and about each other.

When the tour operators and promoters arrived and saw the broken glass of the tour bus they immediately called the police. Everyone involved with the tour was now surrounding our bus. It was so embarrassing. When the police arrived the tour operator told them they wanted to press charges, because they rented the buses. They will be responsible for any damages. He pointed to Cal and said, "He's the one that destroyed my bus."

The policeman walked over to Cal and asked him to put his hands behind his back.

"Last Horizon is fired from the Hot Jamz tour," the tour operator said as he looked from us to Teresa.

As the policeman walked Cal to the car he went on a rant, screaming and accusing Teresa for what had just happened. "You don't want me to tell the police how you hired a hit on my father for the insurance money. How you living, Ma? How you get that house and those cars? Tell'em Ma! Tell'em! Tell them about the drug deals!"

"Shut the hell up, Cal, you're crazy and you're delusional. And the drugs? Do you mean the drugs that you're addicted to? You're a fucking retard, dude," Teresa yelled back at him as the policeman puts him in the car.

When Teresa got angry, she acted out like a true gangster. I'm in total awe. I couldn't believe what just took place so quickly. Just like that we were fired from the tour. Even though we only had a couple weeks left, I could still use that money.

The tour promoter demanded that we get all of our belongings off of the bus. Matt, Teresa, Kev, and I got a taxi and headed to a hotel for the night.

Teresa called an emergency meeting when we got to the hotel. She told us that Cal is mentally sick. She reassured us the things he said are not true and that he makes these things up. I knew that Teresa was once married to Cal's deceased father, but I never had the balls to ask them what happened to him. The most I knew about him was from the family picture they have in the living room at their house. He was a big, tall, serious looking guy with an ugly tattoo of a snake on his hands. Cal never spoke of him and neither did Teresa. I didn't want to hit a soft spot with them so I didn't bother to ask.

She told us that she would let him sit in jail for the night and we will get him in the morning before we get on a plane to Atlanta. Afterwards, Teresa seemed very emotional about what just happened. Though she had a gangster moment she didn't seem as strong as she had been in past altercations. The whole night I kept replaying what happened in my head. The things that Cal said about Teresa stood out to me.

The next day we woke up to calls from many different radio and news stations wanting to get the scoop of why Last Horizon was fired from the Hot Jamz Tour. Teresa instructed us to not answer anything until she spoke with Elite Records. She wanted to explain what happened to them before the media took hold of it.

She told Elite the whole thing was an accident and blown way out of proportion. She was good at coming up with lies to protect the deal we had. On that same call, one of the record company executives told Teresa that the album was underperforming in sells and we will have to negotiate a third single very soon. News like this is only going to help us if we use the bad press to sell our album.

Later that morning we went down to the police station to pick up Cal before we headed to the airport. When we saw Cal he didn't speak to any of us. He seemed to still be pissed about what happened the previous night. When we arrived to the airport there were some paparazzi waiting for us. Of course, they were asking why we were fired from the Hot Jamz tour. We all walked through them as if we didn't hear a thing.

"Cal, who did you throw through the window," one of the cameramen asked. Cal just bowed his head and kept on walking into the airport.

When we arrived at our gate, we took out time to check the internet to see what was being said about the incident. According to one of the most popular blogs, Cal threw one of the members of the group through the tour bus window after a heated argument. Having us all there with no scratches could easily prove this was a lie. Teresa then told us to tell everyone in the media that it was an innocent accident. In fact, no one was thrown through a window.

When we got back to Atlanta things seemed to get back to normal quickly. Cal and Teresa acted as if nothing ever happened. We were invited to come to Atlanta's most popular radio station, Q-105, to clear up the rumors about the tour bus incident. We assured the fans and others that we were not fighting and never have fought. We told them that the whole window thing was an accident and being fired from the tour was not what we intended to happen. We also assured them that we will make it to the remaining cities at a later date. The fans seemed to have bought the lie.

We began doing lots more "over the phone" radio interviews to clear up the rumors. Doing the interviews gave us more exposure, which helped our single get more and more plays. We were then offered the cover of Urban Heat magazine, discussing the incident and our plans for the future. This whole incident had become bigger than the Leo situation. The tour operators rebutted every lie we told, but the fans wanted to believe our story. They even filed a lawsuit against the group. Though the suit was later settled out of court, it gave us more publicity.

All the other acts on the tour refused to comment on the incident. Some of them even said how much they loved the group and the music. Hopefully that would allow the record company to see that Last Horizon was loved by many people.

Meanwhile, Elite Records called a phone conference with us and Teresa. They told us that the next single from the album will be "Love You Forever". This was one of the ballads on our album that was produced by Maestro. The song talked about loving your significant other forever. I liked the song but definitely didn't expect it to be a single. Neither we nor Teresa agreed with this decision, but Elite was the one financing us so we really didn't have a choice. They also informed us that would be the last single off the album and we needed to begin recording a new project. They told us that we would need to change up the sound on this next album.

From the conversation with Elite, I could tell they were not excited about the next Last Horizon project. It was up to us to get it together and make them believe in us again.

Though the song "Love You Forever" wasn't my favorite, I will admit that the video for it was definitely my favorite. We shot the video in Dunwoody at the very top of the King's building (Concourse at Landmark Center). I have always admired those buildings since I'd moved to Atlanta. We really looked like superstars in that video. There was very little choreography which allowed me to just perform the song. The video was #1 on New Beat and other video countdown shows for weeks. Since we knew this would be our last single for this album, it was important to do as much promotion as possible.

TRACK 13:

It's Not Right But It's Okay

It was mid-August and since we were not on tour, we decided to create our very own "Back-To-School" tour. With this tour we would go to many high schools in the country to speak to the students, encouraging them to stay in school while still promoting the album. This tour seemed like a joke at first but once we got it started it was great. We had hundreds of high schools calling us, begging for us to come to their school. By late September, we caught the attention of ASTV and they wanted to become a sponsor for the tour. With ASTV behind the tour, many other major acts were joining us.

Things were going so good at this time. There were fewer arguments in our camp and we all were definitely getting along again. Our single "Love You Forever" was doing really well on radio and video countdowns. Elite Records called us to congratulate us on our album being Platinum.

This was the best news I've ever heard in a long time. All the bad times; fights, tears, long rehearsals, sleepless nights, and relentless touring was all worth it. At least it seemed to be worth it until they pissed me off again. But I believe the school tour really helped that happen for us.

Even though Last Horizon's first album was Platinum in the first two months of its release, it's still a good thing. There was no doubt in our minds that Elite would keep us around for at least another album.

Working on the group's third album was even more exciting. I felt comfortable stepping into the studio because now I was a Platinum

Recording Artist. I felt like everything I touched would turn into platinum. The group was getting offers to collaborate with other major acts. We received one offer from "Traits of Havoc", which was a rap group who sold millions of albums. They were on hiatus for a few years but were returning to the music industry. They wanted me to sing the chorus on their first single back from their hiatus. They specifically asked for me, and me only to come and record with them. They didn't want the rest of the guys. Their manager said that the group liked my voice and thought it would be perfect for their single.

Though I thought this was a good business decision for me as an artist, Teresa and Kev were totally against it. Teresa said that she wanted the group's name in the credits at least, which I understood. Traits of Havoc felt like having Last Horizon's name on the credits would probably make the song seem "bubble gum" and people wouldn't take it as serious. They were famous for making Hip Hop music that delivered a serious world message regarding; politics, poverty, peace, etc. Kev felt like I didn't earn that privilege to sing a song with Traits of Havoc. He felt like this would make me feel as if I didn't need the group and would eventually lure me to go solo.

While I did see what point he was trying to make, I felt like he should have been happy for me. I sang our entire album while they still collected the same amount of pay I did.

I felt like I carried this group on my back when it came to talent. I do give the guys in the group credit for being in rehearsals and on stage with me. But when it came to the actual recording process, they were rarely around to even support me while I'm recording. I felt like I was their engine and they were simply the framework. Cal and Matt both supported my feelings about this offer. They thought it would still be a good thing, for not only me but the group as well. They genuinely felt like I deserved it. This situation ended in a heated discussion amongst us and Teresa, but ultimately Teresa was the boss and she decided to pass on the song with "Traits of Havoc".

I was extremely disappointed in Teresa at that moment. I felt like she truly did not have my best interest at heart. I wasn't sure or clear on why she didn't allow me to. I didn't understand what it was that Kev had against me. I was definitely starting to see those "jealous" traits that Leo had spoken about in the media. I knew from then that I will probably never grow from this group situation. I would probably always do the work while the other guys lip synced to my own background vocals. But this was the deal I signed into. I knew this was still part of my dream but I knew that this situation wasn't going to last for me.

In between this time, we also received many other offers for me to guest star on many TV and movie roles, but they all were denied by Teresa. Several months later, "Traits of Havoc" made their highly anticipated return to the music industry with their first single staying #1 for two months and selling over two million copies online. Wow... Great job Teresa!

TRACK 14:
I Ain't Mad At Cha

At the beginning of recording the group's third album we of course worked with Maestro. Since the release of my first album with the group I turned against Maestro. I felt like he used me and manipulated me in the beginning of everything. He still wanted me to mess around with him and got pissed because I rejected him. I felt nasty, so I told him that I would expose him to Teresa. But he told me that Teresa already knows about him and me. This totally confused me. I didn't believe him, though, because I don't think Teresa would have allowed that to go on.

Even though she didn't allow me to record with "Traits of Havoc", I felt like she was still a bit protective of us. She wouldn't condone anything like what happened between me and Maestro. Like everything else, I brushed it under the rug and continued to work with Maestro on recording the album. Because I rejected him, he would try to convince Teresa that I wasn't focused enough to record this next album. He would play her some of the unfinished work that really didn't sound that good. He even tried to get me replaced on a couple different occasions. He would bring guys to the house and have them audition for her. I privately explained to Teresa, that the songs Maestro was now producing for us were not good and that his sound was outdated.

Maestro's antics back fired when Teresa fired him from being our Executive Producer for our next album. I finally felt like Teresa was hearing me. I felt like she trusted my word. At least I thought she did. But being under pressure from the record company, urging us to change our sound on this next album, Teresa knew that the next album had to be different. Though Maestro is a great producer, he had a signature sound that was getting old. Maestro didn't take being fired lightly. He threatened to expose secrets to the media about the group. To smooth things over Teresa promised to give him at least a one song placement on the next album.

Weeks later Teresa set me up with "Levey", which was a new up and coming producer in Atlanta. If SupaBass was the hottest producer now, Levey would be next in line. He already had placements on the radio and on other artists' albums.

Working with Levey allowed me to be more creative. He was open to my ideas since he was new to the camp. We would stay in the studio for long hours creating songs. Teresa and the other guys would stop in every now and then to see what we had come up with. She felt like we were on a good track to making some good "album fillers", (which are the songs on the album that aren't meant to be singles but take up space on the album). Even though the record company wasn't expecting to hear any of the album for a few months, I wanted to also create songs with hopes of selling them to other artists.

One night while recording I received a text from Marcel saying, "I just want to be a man about this and tell you that I've been dating David for a couple months, and things are getting serious."

I was immediately confused. I didn't even know what "David" he was speaking of. I had to re-read that text message about five times before I was able to understand what he was saying. I guess I didn't want to believe it. I texted him back, "Wow, thanks for telling me."

He texted me back, "I didn't want you to find out no other way, so I felt that I should just tell you myself. Are you ok?"

I texted back, "Yes, I'm fine and I wish the both of you the best. David is a great guy so treat him well."

I wasn't sure how to take this news. I was confused on how they would have even met. But then it dawned on me, I introduced them the day we went and had dinner. But I never seen them exchange numbers or even seen them making any obvious eye contact. My mind was racing and very confused that I couldn't finish recording that night.

Though I believed they would make a nice couple I almost felt betrayed, though I appreciate him for letting me know. How did the person I cheated with end up with the person I cheated on? Hold up, isn't Marcel HIV positive?!

Now I'm wondering if Marcel had even told David about his status. I'm sure he didn't have the balls to tell David about the fling we had, because I know David wouldn't go for that. And knowing how extra careful David was in our relationship I know he couldn't have known about Marcel's status. David made sure we got tested EVERY three months in our relationship. Though David and I were not together any more, I still had very deep feelings for him. I had to talk to him about this.

I debated in my mind if I should ask Marcel if he told David about his status. I didn't want to offend Marcel, even though I should probably be the one that's offended. Marcel had become a good friend that I did begin to trust. But David was my love and deep down I wanted for us to have a future together.

I decided that I had to find a way to tell David myself. I knew he didn't know and it would make me feel like crap if Marcel infected him and I knew about it. This was a tough decision but I had to do what was on my heart and that was to set up a private meeting with David.

The very next day after rehearsals and group meetings, I texted David telling him that it was very important that I speak with him face-to-face. After a couple hours he finally responded and told me to come to his apartment later and we could talk then. I felt like he already knew what I wanted to talk about, and that was him and Marcel being a couple. But that definitely wasn't the only thing. I wanted to know if he knew that Marcel was HIV positive. It wasn't my intention to hurt anyone but this situation could get fatal if I don't speak up.

Later that day I went to David's apartment. After small talking about what was going on in the group and his work life, I gathered the balls to ask him. "So you're seeing Marcel?" I asked.

"Ummm... Yes we are dating. He told me he spoke to you about it already," he replied.

"Yes, he did. I was and I'm still in a bit of shock about it," I said.

"Well, we didn't start talking the day we all met up for dinner that night. We actually ran into each other at a night club. We knew each other looked familiar and we began talking from there," he explained.

"Wow, well what do you know about him?" I asked.

"I know he's a good guy... I'm sorry Juan. I know this situation is more than awkward," he said.

Right then I knew Marcel hadn't told David about his status. Or, maybe David didn't think I knew of Marcel's status and he's not going to volunteer that information to me. Feeling a bit anxious and frustrated I just came out with it. "Do you know that Marcel is HIV positive?" I blurted out.

The room became very quiet. I swear the entire Earth stopped moving for a few seconds. David looked stunned at what I just said. He put his hands over his mouth in shock and tears began to fall from his eyes. Feeling a bit guilty for spilling the beans I rushed to hug him. "I'm so sorry. I'm so sorry," I repeated. "I really care for you, David, and I just thought you should know."

David was silent, not saying a word, just crying. I pulled him away to see his face and it was filled with tears.

"Are you okay," I asked.

"I think so Juan," he said, trembling. "I just want you to know that I already knew Marcel's status. He told me when we first started talking. I'm just so hurt because I didn't want you to find out like this, but I'm also HIV positive."

I felt like I was in a matrix. This was not happening. This could not be real. David was so careful about everything he did. Oh my God, what if I had HIV and just hadn't showed any symptoms? My mind was racing and I felt like I had to vomit.

After David had calmed down, he began to explain that he and Marcel didn't really meet at a night club, but at a HIV clinic. They both learned of their statuses almost around the same time. I was numb. I didn't know what to think or how to feel. "Why didn't you tell me?" I asked.

"I was scared and didn't know how you would react to me," he said.

"How did this happen to you?" I asked.

"After we broke up, I was devastated. I felt lost. I was so used to us being together. I felt lonely and I felt like you no longer cared. I began drinking and partying a lot to make myself feel better. And I slept around... I wasn't careful. I regret it. I was being stupid. I didn't love me because I loved you and..." he said but paused.

"I'm so sorry, David," I said. I gave him a tight hug and I didn't want to let him go. I felt like I played a part in his condition, though I knew deep down it wasn't my fault. I still had so much love for David and now I could only be there for him as much as possible.

I sat and talked to David for a couple hours that day. Eventually we both cheered up a bit and began talking about other things. I felt like I needed to really educate myself on HIV/AIDS because I knew very little about it. All I knew is you can get it from having unprotected sex and lots of people have died from it. David did tell me that his health is up and down. He took about 3 pills twice a day to handle the symptoms.

Leaving David's house that night I felt like my life had again changed. Or maybe it was just my perspective. I could not believe what was happening around me. My life was never this complicated. The whole ride home I cried. Even though David was on medication, I just felt like he would die soon. And even though that might not be true, it felt like a part of him died within me. He was no longer the same person he was before I joined the group.

Though I enjoyed the recognition from being in the group I honestly was very unhappy. I really didn't have any real friends or anybody who truly cared for me in that situation. The person that I knew that cared the most was going through something we both did so much to protect ourselves from. And Marcel, my friend, was now in a relationship with the only person that cared for me. I felt like I had no one really to turn to. My family back home in Illinois wouldn't understand

what I was going through. They loved seeing me on TV so much, I don't

think they'd believe me if I told them the truth anyway. This was all too

stressful.

TRACK 15:
They Don't Care About Us

In the next coming months we were still promoting the school tour, making appearances and setting up for the next album. The Grammy Awards had come and went without us even getting one nomination. This didn't sit well with the record company. We all were expecting it, but it didn't happen. Us not even being nominated for a Grammy became headlines in some urban magazines. This added so much pressure on Teresa and the group because we really felt this album would take the group further than the last. We knew that Elite Records would count this as a failure even if we did sell over a million copies. Going Platinum for them was an expectation from all of their artists, not much of an accomplishment.

Elite Records wanted to begin the process on the next album so they called a meeting with us in LA.

During the meeting we played everything I recorded with Levey and Maestro. While they said the work sounded good, they said we had no singles. They didn't feel like any of the songs were worthy of being played on the radio. This reminded me of the last album's review. We were at least hoping that they will give us a bigger budget for the album and set us up with SupaBass again, but no. They told us all to our faces that they've decided to drop us from the label. Last Horizon had become a liability to Elite Records. They had spent more money on the production of videos, albums, and promotion than they've supposedly profited.

When it came to the actual financials Teresa was sure that we stayed in the dark about most of it. I never knew how much we actually made from selling albums because Teresa collected all royalties on the group's behalf. I learned later that I signed over all of my creative rights to Teresa. Even if I wrote a book she was still entitled to collect royalties. She owned it all and it was all written in the contract that I ignorantly signed.

Teresa and the guys seemed heartbroken over being dropped from Elite Records. They felt like it was over for us but deep down I was happy about it. I felt like I touched a part of my dream and for that I was thankful. I was ready to move on with life and away from them.

When we got back to the hotel that night Teresa didn't say much at all. All four of us tried to cheer her up. Kev blamed it all on me. He says that it's my fault the last album didn't do as good as they did when Leo was in the group. I was so hurt by that that I didn't have the energy to fight back with him. I allowed him to say and believe whatever he wanted. When it came to Kev, I was emotionally burnt out with him. Anything that he had to say didn't matter to me. Matt and Cal both reassured me that Kev was a bit full of himself and if it wasn't for me, the group would have been done over a year ago.

Having those two to stand up for me really made me feel good. I believe they really did appreciate the hard work I did for the group. They both truly understood their actual roles versus mine.

TRACK 16:
Don't Stop
Believin'

When we got back to Atlanta, Teresa was franticly trying to reach out to other record labels that would be interested in signing us. She wanted to find us another deal before our being dropped by Elite hit the press. If the media found out, other record companies will feel like they're taking a huge risk by signing a previously signed "unsuccessful" act.

After speaking with a few record labels that day she called me into her room alone. She told me that she wanted me to fly out to New

York to meet with her good friend Michael G. of Hit Maker Records. She told me that he would consider having us signed to his label but he wanted to see how I worked in the studio. I've only been to New York a few times, and I wasn't comfortable going alone.

"Well can't the other guys go with me?" I asked feeling confused.

"No, Juan he only wants you. He wants you... So you got to take one for the team. I'll make sure you'll get a bigger advance," she said.

"What do you mean, 'one for the team'?" I asked.

"You know. I'm glad we're having this conversation. Maestro told me everything. Don't act like you don't get down with dudes. Michael G. likes guys like you and he wants to work with you in New York. We need this; you need this. We are all depending on *you* Juan. So you're just going to give up everything you've worked for? It's nothing to sleep with someone for what you want. It's your fault we lost our deal with Elite in the first place, to be honest. You owe it to the guys, you owe this to us," she said.

At that point I was so confused and I couldn't believe that Teresa is pimping me out for a record deal. I knew she could be low down but this had to be the lowest. She knew what to say to tug at my emotions and she mentally raped me once again.

Feeling like; maybe it was my fault the group lost its deal, I agreed to fly to New York the next day. I felt like I just made yet another deal with the devil. I was digging myself so many holes that I would probably live to regret. I was raised to have way more dignity and pride than this. There is no way I would ever tell anyone about these things. I was so ashamed of myself but I also knew that if I was going to New York alone to secure us a deal I could also secure me a solo deal for the future. Being alone would allow me to talk about what I wanted without Teresa's supervision.

Being in New York for the first time without Teresa and the guys actually felt good. I felt a sense of freedom. I was going to be there for a full week to hang out with Michael G. and record a couple songs with his producers, making sure we could get a deal.

Michael G. was very suave and smooth. He had lots of women around all the time. He even had one of his women to pick me up from the airport. One particularly caught my attention and her name was Nicky. She was really cool and easy to talk to. She was trying to be an artist herself and was trying to get signed to Hit Maker Records. She wrote one of the songs I recorded for Last Horizon's potential album with Hit Makers.

The studio sessions went extremely well and Michael G. seemed to be very pleased with the songs that were being recorded.

He took me back to his condo and we sat out on the balcony facing the brightly lit concrete jungle of New York City. He seemed very easy to talk to. He asked me very deep personal questions about the group and Teresa. Feeling like this could be a trap; I made sure I said positive things about them. I didn't want to get caught in the middle of any drama with Teresa and the guys.

"So would you ever consider going solo?" he asked.

I hesitated, "I don't know if I would be ready for that," I said. I was trying to be modest but in my mind I was saying, "It's about time, I thought you'd never ask."

"Well I'll be honest to say that you carry Last Horizon. Without you they would be nothing. I got the power to make stars. And you are the star of that group. I understand Teresa wants to keep the group going and as a friend I'm willing to help out as much as I can... I guess. But honestly, this is the last horizon for Last Horizon. So soak it up as much as you can because I'm going to make *YOU* big," he said as he lit a cigar.

To hear him say that felt amazing. I felt like Teresa's plan of pimping me just turned into what she really didn't want to happen. "So you don't think Last Horizon can survive another album?" I asked him.

"I think Teresa destroyed that group when she created it. And this is just between me and you. She put that group together to cover up a lot of her dirt. I've known Teresa for many, many years and I'm sure Last Horizon is a financial cover up," he said, puffing his cigar.

"A cover up? How so? I don't think so, and I should know I'm around her every day, all day," I said, laughing.

I was playing dumb and innocent so that he'll keep talking. I had already become suspicious of Teresa and how she's been able to maintain her lavish lifestyle but I'm not 100% sure of anything.

"Juan, man, you are a good kid with a clean record. You're living your dreams and I'm sure you're not paying attention to everything that's around you. I'm sure for you this all happened so fast. Keep your eyes peeled. Pay attention... Like I said, I'm going to do what I can for you boys but..."

He never finished that statement. I didn't know what to think. Once again someone was telling me to be careful of Teresa. I've seen and had my taste of her wickedness but what else could there be? Michael G. is really good friends with Teresa and he would have no reason to lie on her. Even her own son had blurted out foul things about her. What could be so bad that no one will tell me exactly what it is? I appreciate him giving me a heads up though. After he finished his cigar, we both went in and drank a bottle of some expensive champagne. Michael G. is normally very suave and laid back but when he gets some alcohol in him he does get loose. He began flirting with me and knowing my mission I flirted back. I have never been submissive and thankfully Michael was because even though I was interested in guys I didn't have those desires.

The next day I was back in the studio working with Nicky. We really got along really good. We exchanged numbers and promised to keep in touch. We went out to lunch together where we talked about everything under the sun. I felt like I knew her from a past life or something. She understood my struggles and I understood hers. She told me lots of things about her past that really made me feel comfortable with her. Nicky is definitely the type of girl that I would be in a relationship with.

Michael G. didn't seem to mind how close we were getting at all. I guess as long as he was getting what he wanted, it didn't matter much to him. Even though we were getting close really fast over that week I would never reveal my sexuality to anyone. Though she had told me lots about her sexual past with other women, I just couldn't allow myself to be that open. I wasn't in the business of admitting to anything. I knew that I was bi-sexual but I also knew a lot of people didn't understand it. And normally what people don't understand, they hate it out of ignorance. But I know I'm a good person that loves God and that's what really matters to me.

The whole time I was in New York, Teresa called and texted me constantly. She wanted to know every detail of me and Michael G.'s interactions and conversations. I made it seem as if we only discussed song concepts and album ideas.

"Don't tell him anything about me. If he asks anything personal about me, tell him 'you don't know.' Don't discuss anything that's happened in my house or my group. If we don't get this deal, it's because of something you did wrong", she texted me one night while I was in New York.

Overall the trip to New York was all bitter sweet. Even though I was sent here to basically prostitute, I also felt like there was a good chance that I'd be able to break away from Teresa. So many times I felt like I should run away but the feelings of failure kept me going. I also began to live in fear of my own life. I couldn't really think of anyone I could run to that would understand. If I left the group at this point it would get too much media attention. There was no way for me to hide.

I didn't agree with anything I did or said but I knew that one day I would be able to tell this story. I often wondered who else in this business has been through similar situations and was just too afraid to speak up.

If Hell was a real place, I'm sure I was living close to its' neighborhood. I felt like more and more of myself was dying every day. I could feel death in the air. The feeling was strong and I could sense that things were about to change dramatically. After all I've done, I could only hope and pray that God still loved me.

Getting back to Atlanta, I was depressed. In my mind I was trying to plot and plan my way out of this situation with the group and still have a career in music. I played the songs we recorded for the guys and Teresa and they weren't so pleased. She called Michael G. to have a conference call about what his vision was and if he felt he could sign the group.

Michael G. indeed wanted to sign the group to a new five album deal. A five album record deal is almost standard in the recording business. Most artists don't last long enough to fulfill this contractual obligation. Though Teresa and the guys were excited once again, I pretended to be happy. I knew before I left New York he would sign us, I also knew that he may be interested in signing me to a solo deal. I figured if I just played the role, my day will come.

Michael G. told Teresa that our new single will be one of the songs that I recorded while I was in New York called, "Fast Lane". Even though Teresa said she didn't like any of the songs I recorded in New York, she pretended to be excited about this decision.

"Fast Lane" was an up-tempo club type of song that talks about living a fast sexual life. Since I now knew two people who I cared about with HIV, this message wasn't appealing to me. Even though I didn't like the message, it was just a song and this was indeed my job. Michael G.

said that he would leak the song to New York radio and see how people like it before we shot a video and began a radio tour to promote it.

Now that we had a new record deal we were able to speak about it publically. The media didn't seem to care much that we were signed to Hit Maker Records, they loved that we were dropped from Elite Records though.

"Fast Lane" did well in New York so Michael G. decided to leak it to other radio stations around the country. Our fans didn't take so well to the song because they felt like the message wasn't our type of thing. They saw us as a clean-cut type of group. But DJs and people that are regular clubbers seemed to love it. Since the song was starting to pick up spins on the radio, Michael G. flew us all out to New York to his office for a conference meeting with his staff to discuss our next album, budget, and to give us advances. When it came to getting a check, Teresa made sure she was first in line. I was curious to see if she would hold up her end of the bargain and give me a bigger cut of the advance, or at least a tip for my troubles.

TRACK 17:

Mo' Money, Mo' Problems

When we landed In New York, Michael G. had one of his drivers to pick us up from the airport in a black, fully tented SUV. Elite has never picked us up from the airport. Michael G. knew how to treat his artist like stars. The driver dropped us off at an expensive hotel that was only three blocks away from Hit Maker offices. After we checked in at the hotel, which was paid for by Hit Makers, we had about an hour to spare before our big meeting. Everyone was in good spirits. Teresa was extra nice to all of us even Cal. In the midst of good feelings Cal decided to help his mom take her luggage up to her room. She always over packed her three Louis Vuitton duffle bags when we went places. Even though this may seem like a simple gesture, it was a milestone for them two. Teresa instructed us to go to our rooms to freshen up and to meet in the lobby in about thirty minutes.

After about fifty-five minutes Cal, Kev, Matt and I were waiting in the lobby of the hotel for Teresa to come down. We were always waiting on Teresa. She had her own sense of time which caused us to be late for almost everything.

Our meeting with Hit Maker was set for eleven o' clock. It was now ten fifty-six. Even though our hotel was only about 3 blocks away from where Hit Maker was situated, I felt like we should have been there at least twenty to thirty minutes early for a meeting this important. But Teresa has a mentality that people should bend and fold to accommodate her. Since she and Michael G. are friends, she probably didn't think he'd mind. We all started to get worried that we'd be late. We all agreed that Cal would call her cell phone to let her know that we were waiting for her downstairs in the lobby. Neither one of us wanted to call her because we were afraid she'd feel like we were trying to tell her what to do. If she ever felt threaten in any way she was sure to use her petty tactics to regain her control. Since she and Cal seemed to be having a good day, we nominated him. He patted himself down and realized that he'd left his phone and wallet in her room when he helped her take her luggage up. He immediately jumped up and headed to the elevator to go retrieve his things.

Just as he made his way to the beautiful glass elevator doors, we could see that Teresa was just about to get off. Just as the elevator doors opened, he asked Teresa for her spare key so he could get his things. This caused another heated feud between Cal and Teresa. Knowing that this feud was going to get ugly Kev, Matt and I ran toward the elevators to help defuse the altercation.

"Why didn't you think of that 20 minutes ago?" Teresa asked as she pulled out her room key.

"I was helping you out, we're already going to be late because of you," Cal said loudly, causing other people in the lobby to turn and look at us.

"Look we can't do this here or now, we have to have our energy right for this meeting," Matt said as he stepped in between Teresa and Cal.

I was actually impressed with how Matt stepped up and said something. He usually just looks away and pretends nothing is happening. But Last Horizon's current situation was a life or death situation. This meeting could be our last. Matt grabbed the room key from Teresa and handed it to Cal.

"And hurry up, you retarded ass bastard," Teresa said harshly and partially under her breath.

Cal just looked at her and didn't say a word. I could tell he was hurt and wanted to say something back but for the sake of everyone else, he held his tongue. By the time Cal came back downstairs, we were already running about five minutes late.

When we arrived at the Hit Maker Records office our energy was just as uncertain and dark as the black leather furniture and décor in their office. Even the walls were painted black with hundreds of platinum album plats spread throughout. It was apparent that an altercation amongst us had just occurred. No one was saying anything, probably because Teresa told us to not say anything. She took total control in situations like these, she was afraid that we'd say something to jeopardize our opportunities.

The front desk receptionist rang Michael G. and told him that we had just arrived. She pointed us to the conference room where our meeting was to be held.

When we walked in the room Michael G. and five people from his staff were in the conference room sitting around a long black table. They all looked like they were not pleased with our tardiness. They looked at us the same way the guys and Teresa looked at me when I walked into that room to audition for them. "So this is part of the reason why Last Horizon isn't selling records. You guys don't know how to be professional enough to show up on time. My time is money. My staff's time is money. I have thousands of starving artists out there that would love to have a meeting with me and my staff. But Last Horizon is so BIG that they make the CEO wait? No. This will never happen again. Now sit," Michael G. said demandingly as we took our seats around the long black table. I was surprised that Teresa didn't say anything inappropriate back to Michael G. I guess she knew when to shut up. He seemed very different from the person I spent an entire week with. He was very direct and to the point. I tried to make eye contact with him to see if we still had a deal on my future solo projects. He wasn't budging he was all about the business with Last Horizon at that moment.

I couldn't help but wonder why he still considered doing business with Teresa if he knew she was up to no good. I just couldn't totally wrap my mind around the depths of their relationship. Maybe he was somehow tangled in the same black widow's web that I was.

In the conference we discussed the next moves for the group which seemed promising but a lot slower than Elite Records. He didn't want for us to release an album until he has his staff try to promote "Fast Lane". Though he set Teresa a budget for production on the next album he insisted that we don't shoot a video for "Fast Lane". He wanted to see if this would be a single that could potentially sell this next album.

"Fast Lane may not even make this album. It may be just a song that keeps Last Horizon on the radio and current," he told us.

Though Teresa agreed, I knew deep down she really didn't agree. But having those checks in her hands made her happy. We signed that deal with Hit Maker Records without any consultation from a lawyer. I guess Teresa really trusted Michael G. or maybe it was his money she trusted.

We left that meeting feeling as uncertain as we came. It was a good thing that the group now had a new deal, but Michael G. didn't seem to really know what to do with us. Even though he gave Teresa a budget and a fifty thousand dollar advance for the group, it just didn't feel like a moment to celebrate. I only knew the amount of this advancement because Michael G. mentioned it as we all signed his contract. If they were not friends I'm sure he wouldn't release any money to her.

Michael G. was under the impression that the songs that I recorded in New York were the beginning of us recording this album. Teresa told us not to mention that we already recorded the album, which was the album that was rejected by Elite Records. So the production budget and advance that Michael G. gave to Teresa will go directly into her pockets. All while she presents him with the same songs that I recorded for the album that was rejected by Elite.

Since the production for those songs were already paid for, and she had bought all rights to them, she felt confident that those songs were at least good enough for Michael G. to approve for the next album. Teresa was smart but very dirty. I felt like I was finally understanding how Teresa's mind worked. She was extremely money hungry and always finding ways to get over on the next person.

Later that night, Cal and I went down to Times Square to hang out before we headed back to Atlanta the next day. The others went back to the hotel for the night. While we were out walking through Times Square, Cal began to open up to me about how he felt about his mom. He just came right out with it.

"Everything I do is to please her and I try so hard to make her happy. My whole life she's made me feel invisible. Though I was her only child, she always put other people before me. My dad left us when I was about five and I've never heard from him. I honestly don't remember what he looks like. She burned all the pictures we had of him. I feel like my mom blamed me for him leaving. She would beat me for no reason at times. There were times when she would beat me till she seen blood. I would go to school with swollen, busted lips and I would lie to my teachers and say I fell or something.

"When my mom met Richard, my 'other dad', things had gotten so much better. She seemed to be happy again. I loved Richard. He treated me like his real son", he said.

"So Richard is the guy in the picture with you and Teresa, with the tattoo of a snake on his hand? What happened to him?" I asked.

"Yea, that's Richard... I hated his tattoo. One day I came home from school and the house was a mess. There was broken glass and all the furniture was flipped over. It looked like a hurricane happened in the house. When I walked into the living room I seen my mom just standing there looking dazed. She told me to do her a favor and go to my friend's house down the street until she called me to come home. I was scared and I knew something wasn't right. I just ran out the house and went to my friend's house.

"When I got to my friend's house my mom called and asked his mom if I could stay with them for a few hours. She said she had to run some important errands. I was so uneasy that I just sat and stared out the window. My friend and his mom both kept asking me if was I okay and I ensured them both that I was.

"While I was there I seen my dad drive past in his car towards our house. Then about 30 minutes later I saw my mom driving past with a man in the passenger seat of her car going in the opposite direction. I couldn't see who the man was because of the tint on her windows but I know I seen someone else with her. Then about ten minutes later I heard fire and police sirens. When I looked out the window I seen fire trucks and police headed into the direction of our house.

"I immediately knew they were going to my house, so I ran out of my friend's house and headed home. I couldn't believe my eyes. Our entire house was on fire. I could do nothing but cry as my friend and his mom chased after me. My friend's mom held me and told me that everything was going to be okay but I knew it wasn't."

"When my mom showed up she was hysterical, or at least she pretended to be. She kept screaming, 'My husband is in there! My husband is in there.' I felt at that moment she had hired someone to kill my dad and she staged this entire thing. Later they found his remains in the living room burned to the bone. I've been through a lot, man," he explained as we continued to walk.

I was floored about what he had just told me. I was seriously speechless. I knew Teresa was hardcore but this was beyond that. Teresa was a true gangster. Not the gang sign, bandana wearing type of gangster. She was the chop your body up and feed it to the sharks type of gangster. Knowing this made me now fear her. It was a deep thick dark fear that I felt with every beat of my heart.

TRACK 18:
When It All Falls Down

When Cal and I arrived back to our room that night he unsuccessfully tried to open the door with his room key. He realized that it was Teresa's spare key that he had gotten from her earlier that day. "Go ahead and use your key while I take this key back to my mom's room," he said as he walked only about three doors down.

I pulled out my key and opened the door to our room and went inside. I went to sit on the bed when I heard a loud scream and it sounded like Teresa. I could also hear Cal yelling. I ran out of the room to Teresa's room to find Cal on top of Kev beating him in the face.

Teresa and I were able to pull Cal off Kev. Kev's face was pouring with blood as if Cal had cut him with something. He was wrapped up in the sheet and I can tell that he was completely naked underneath. Teresa only had on a bra and panties. I'm so confused on what's going on.

Cal was still trying to jump over me and get to Kev while yelling, "This bitch is fucking my mom!"

Teresa began slapping and yelling at Cal.

"Yea, I'm your new daddy bitch!", Kev yells to Cal.

Cal then picked up a lamp and took a good swing at Kev's head but ended up hitting him on the neck which left a big, ugly permanent bruise.

Suddenly Cal dropped the lamp and stormed out.

"Get the hell out!" Teresa yelled to me.

I immediately left and went back to my room. I thought Cal would be there, but he wasn't. I figured he went outside to cool down. I just stood there stunned for about ten minutes. I couldn't believe what just happened and all so quickly.

I called Matt and Kev's room to talk to Matt and see if he heard what was going on. He said he heard a commotion but didn't think much of it, which is understandable since their room was further down the end of the hall. I asked him to come to my room and he did.

I explained to him what had just happened and he told me he knew that Kev and Teresa were messing around. He said they have been messing around since Leo was in the group. Matt was great at keeping secret.

I couldn't believe how this was going on so long and Cal didn't know about it. I was so uncomfortable. I'm not sure how to act or treat Teresa and Kev. I knew this would change us forever.

I didn't think Cal would want to be around Kev now that this had happened, but this sort of explained Kev's behavior towards me and why he was against me doing things outside the group.

It also explained why Teresa was conflicted about allowing me to do so. She was trying to protect Kev's feeling by doing what he wanted her to do.

After Matt left my room, I tried to call over to Teresa's room and see if I could privately speak to her. I also wanted to make sure she was okay at least, but she never answered the phone. I also called and texted Cal's cell phone, but he didn't reply at all. I figured that he'd be back later. I'm sure he wanted to go blow off some steam. I stayed up for hours waiting for Cal to get back.

He came back around four in the morning. He was drunk. I'd never seen him this type of drunk. He seemed to barely keep his balance. He smelled like smoke and I could tell that he had smoked something as well.

"Oh, you're still up?" he asked me as he stumbled to his bed.

"Yeah, man, you okay?" I asked.

"No, I'm not okay. My mom is not what she may seem to be Juan. I shouldn't tell you but you're going to find out eventually. She had my father killed for lots of insurance money to pay off a huge debt that she owed a big drug dealer here in New York. She killed him for money. Last Horizon is just a cover up so that she can make money from her drug deals and not be questioned by the Feds. If they see that she's managing and housing a famous pop group they will think that her money is coming from record sells, tours, and other things regarding the group. So they won't bother to audit her. How do you think she got those cars and that house? I love my mother, but she's dirty. I'm sorry, Juan," he slurred.

I was frozen listening to him expose more of the truth. He stopped talking and dozed off to sleep. I was not able to sleep at all. I was now very scared. I didn't know what tomorrow was going to bring.

I was sure Teresa would keep the group going based off what Cal just said, but how? Maybe Cal and Kev will just get along for the sake of the group. I knew that tomorrow was going to be an extreme challenge. But this too shall pass— Hopefully.

When the sun rose that morning I jumped in the shower and prepared to leave the hotel. Cal was still sleep. I knew he would be hung over but I was willing to help him as much as he needed. After I got out the shower I called down to Matt's room to see if he was getting ready. I called down to Teresa's room and she finally answered. She told me to make sure everyone meets in the hotel lobby in about an hour. I could tell from her voice that she had probably been up all night. She explained that what I saw was not what it looked like or what Cal tried to make it seem. I knew she was lying because Matt confirmed the truth to me last night.

After I gathered my things I went over to Cal's bed and tried to shake him to wake him up. I kept calling his name and shaking him but he didn't seem to be responding. I knew he was drunk when he came in so I expected that waking him up wouldn't be easy.

I continued to shake him when I felt how cold his body was. And I noticed that he wasn't breathing. I shook him harder. I began to panic and scream his name. I screamed for Teresa as I rushed out of the room.

She busted out of her room and ran to ours. I was sure she could tell by my scream that something was really wrong.

"Cal, Cal, Cal... he won't wake up," I cried.

She screamed as she began trying to shake and wake him up. "Call 911," she yelled to me.

I grabbed the phone and did as she asked. This seemed like a bad dream that you try to wake up from but can't. It was like I was paralyzed within myself. I couldn't grasp this reality. This just didn't seem to be happening. I called Matt and Kev down to the room. Moments later the hotel manager arrived. He was trying his best to help us calm Teresa down.

When the paramedics arrived they tried performing CPR to revive him but nothing worked. They pronounced him dead at the scene. The police questioned me about his behavior when he came in last night. All I could tell them and Teresa is that he came in drunk, he laid down and went to sleep. I didn't know what else to say. I wasn't going to reveal what he told me before he fell asleep though.

We later found out that Cal died from a ruptured brain aneurysm, and a possible drug overdose. I knew he was definitely drinking but I didn't think he was doing drugs. I didn't realize how sick he actually was. It was later revealed that Cal was using cocaine and crystal meth. How did I not see this? I guess I'd never really seen anyone on drugs to know what that looks like.

The word of Cal's death got out very fast. It was all over the news and radio. We were getting calls from lots of magazines that wanted to print up a story about his death. My father even called to speak to me and make sure I was okay.

Hearing my father's voice made me feel like it was all worth it. He seemed so human and genuine; I'd never seen this side to him. I felt like Superman had just come to save the day.

"Well that's part of life. People die, son," my father said before we said our good byes.

Knowing that I had my father's support gave me lots of strength to pull through this situation. Teresa instructed us to not talk to the media until we were able to get back home to Atlanta. This was a sad time for us. Even Kev was taking it hard.

Once we got back to Atlanta, Teresa quickly contacted her insurance provider and made funeral arrangements. She even demanded that I sing on behalf of the group at the funeral. I wasn't in the mood to sing at his service but I did it anyway. Seeing Cal lay in his casket didn't seem real at all. I stared at his body as if I was expecting him to move. I watched closely to see if he was breathing, even though I know he wasn't. I just couldn't believe Cal was dead. Lots of fans, other artists and even Michael G. showed up to his funeral to pay their respects.

In my mind the group was over. I couldn't see her wanting to continue the group since she just lost her son. But the night of the funeral she called us all into a meeting where she announced that she wanted to hold auditions to replace Cal.

"Cal would want to see us continue. So in his memory we're going to continue", she said as if she was trying to hold back her tears.

"Why don't we just keep it at three of us", Matt asked concernedly.

"I built this group. Last Horizon was built to be a four man group. My decision is final and not up for discussion. Cal was my son and he understood my vision for this group. Like I said, he would want us to continue", Teresa said firmly.

I couldn't believe what she was saying. Her son was just put in the ground and she was talking about replacing him already. I was outraged in the inside. I appreciated this situation for allowing me to experience my dreams but this was all a nightmare. I had lost so much of myself during this whole time and I just couldn't get the nerve to continue, knowing what I know now.

Since Cal told me exactly what was happening, I would be a fool to stay. Matt can stay all he wants. Kev is going to stay, I'm sure, as long as Teresa would have him. For me, I'm done.

"I can't do this," I told them as I stood up to walk away.

"What do you mean? You have no choice. You will do as I say," Teresa yelled to me.

Matt and Kev both looked confused.

"Leo was lucky to walk away from me. The next person is not walking away from me, Juan. Your only way out is by death," Teresa said.

I turned around to look at her. I could tell by the sound of her voice she was serious. If she was capable of having her husband killed, I'm sure she would have no problem doing me the same.

"I'm sorry, I'm just hurting because I was the one that found Cal," I said slowly, even pretending to get emotional. I just wanted to tell Teresa whatever she wanted to hear. She seemed very satanic at that moment and I didn't want any more problems.

"So, you don't trust me? I do everything for you guys. You live in my house. I feed you. I clothe you. I even gave you a career. You will never make it without me. I made you who you are. Remember that," she said.

The fear of my life had really settled into my spirit. I was officially her slave, at least she thought. Though I played along, I knew that if I ever wanted to still do music that Michael G. would sign me to a solo deal. But honestly, music was the last thing on my mind. I just wanted to get far away from Teresa and Last Horizon.

TRACK 19:

Dance With My Father

A few days after Cal's funeral we received a call from Michael G. wanting us to record a song called "Like Honey" for an upcoming movie soundtrack.

"Like Honey" was written and produced by Michael G.'s own team of writers and producers that were based in Atlanta. Michael G. said that this song also had the potential to be a single for the group. I just couldn't believe that we were moving along so quickly after Cal's death. It just seemed as if they didn't care how the group felt about moving forward without him, it was all about the money.

Right before we entered the studio to record "Like Honey", I received the call from my mom that night that completely changed my entire life. She told me that my father was just in a really bad accident on his motorcycle. She said that there were other people that were hurt as well and that the entire northbound lane of Interstate 57 towards Chicago was closed. I already wasn't feeling like recording because Cal's death was just too fresh in my mind. I almost wished that my mom didn't call me with this news, especially at this time. Now my mind was on my father.

I couldn't think straight but I wanted to get through this recording session. I just hoped he was okay. I quickly thought to go online to see if I could find out more about his accident. I figured if the accident was bad enough to close down the interstate, it would likely make the news. I pulled out my phone while I was in the studio and went to the Chicago local news website and there it was as the headline, "Three People Dead and Others Critically Injured in a Motorcycle Crash on Interstate 57".

My heart pounded harder and harder as I read the article. In the article it didn't mention the names of those that had died. I quickly prayed that maybe he was just one of the "critically injured". I received another call about ten minutes later from my mother, I could tell that she was crying and could barely talk but I heard her say, "he's dead". My mouth opened in complete shock.

My body quickly ejected all the air in my lungs. I felt like Mike Tyson and Muhammad Ali both punched me in the chest at the same time. I fell to my knees and when I finally was able to inhale some air I exhaled the most horrible loudest high pitched scream I had ever heard. I didn't think I had that in me. It was like I was releasing a spirit within me and he was finally setting himself free after millions of years of captivity.

In the midst of my tears and crying Teresa rushed over to hug me. She's tried to figure out what is going on with me. The other guys huddled around to hug me as well. The songwriters and producers of the song all just looked at us in complete silence. They knew this was the first song we were recording after Cal's death, so they probably expected some emotional breakdowns during the session. I was still so shocked that I couldn't really get it out to tell Teresa that my father had died.

Finally I was able to calm down a bit to say, "My father was just killed in a motorcycle accident."

Teresa immediately held me closer. I was thinking for a second that maybe Teresa does have a heart until she whispered in my ear, "I'll allow you to fly home the night before the funeral but you need to be back the night of the funeral."

I couldn't believe this. Here I am having a moment that just completely changed my life and she was going to "allow" me? I said, "No, I'm going home as soon as possible."

Teresa just showed her true colors once again. But honestly, I wasn't too surprised. She was a cold-hearted snake. If she didn't care for her son much, she definitely wasn't going to care for me. She then told me to get myself together because we needed to finish this song tonight. I was so upset that I shut down completely. At that moment I had no care for Last Horizon, I just wanted to go home to Illinois and be with my family.

I apologized to Teresa, Kev, Matt, the songwriters and producers and told them that I was unable to record the song at that time. They all seemed to understand until we were headed to the car and I overheard Teresa telling Kev, "I don't understand how someone could cry so much for someone they barely knew."

"Right", Kev said agreeing with Teresa.

Just to hear her say that made me hurt even more in the inside. She knew how to crush me and she did.

Later that night I booked my own flight to Illinois. I called Marcel and asked if I could leave my car at his house while I was away. We agreed that I would pick him up on my way to the airport and he would take my car back to his house. I didn't bother making arrangements with Teresa. I think she felt like she had to let me go because otherwise would make her seem inhumane. How ironic...

At the time when my father died I felt like I was finally getting the attention from him that I had always desired. The last conversation I had with him he was trying to console me about Cal's death and now he's dead. He said, "Well that's part of life, people die, Son."

I still remember that conversation and I could hear him saying that over and over to me. It's funny how before people die they do things out of the ordinary, or at least it seems. My father came to me just as my mother told he would. I always wondered if he knew he would die soon and he wanted to mend our relationship before he did. Or, does God change people before they die? Whichever way I'm grateful for the times he did call. Even if I didn't get the attention when I wanted or felt I needed it most, I still got it.

When I joined the group and made several media appearances my father then seemed to pay attention. He called me so much at that time that I was overwhelmed with all the attention he was giving me. I didn't know how to handle it. I never experienced it before. Part of me was jumping for joy and the other part was still so angry at him. Whenever he would call, the first thing he would say was, "Hey, Son!" Just to hear him call me his son ignited a new flow of blood through my veins.

My mom always told me that one day he would come around, and when he did to let him in. I was doing just that. I was letting him in and even though I was grown, I still felt like a little kid whenever I spoke to him.

I remember about a month before he died he called me so much to the point I was annoyed. At first I was so excited about the attention he was showing me that I would tell Teresa how happy it made me for him to call. I told Teresa how it was for me growing up without him around much. She made me feel like the only reason why he wanted to come around was because I was in the group. So, I had begun to think that he only wanted to be in my life because he could then brag to his friends about who I was.

I had begun to feel like; as a child I wasn't important enough for any phone calls or "Happy Birthdays" but now you can call all the time? One night, after one of our phone conversations I threw my phone down and said out loud, "Damn, he's getting on my nerves will all these phones calls."

Seconds later I heard him saying, "Hello? Hello?"

I picked up my phone and realized that I hadn't hung up the call with him. I immediately hung up the phone. It hurt me so much to think that he heard what I said, and how me must've felt. I wondered if he felt how I felt my entire life. Hurt. Empty. Lost. Confused. Unwanted. Unappreciated. Unloved.

At my father's funeral I cried so much because I knew there was no way now to completely mend that relationship. I was at a loss my whole life and now it was official. I would never get the chance to have the father and son relationship that I had always dreamed about.

TRACK 20:

A Change Gon' Come

When I got back to Atlanta after my father's funeral my mindset was changing fast. I felt like one of the main reasons why I wanted to be in this group was so that my father would be proud of me. Now that he was gone, I had almost no desire to continue doing music or at least with Last Horizon.

My father was a completely healthy forty-eight-year-old when he died. Cal was very young when he died as well. I began to see how short life could really be. I realized then that we don't have any control over the day we die. Life was way too precious to continue to be manipulated and a slave. I needed to take all control over my life and I was going to do just that.

Getting back to the house with Teresa and the guys was very strange. I felt like I didn't know them anymore. Teresa was upset since I had taken a couple weeks off to be with my family in Illinois. I later found out they actually held a private unsuccessful audition to replace me while I was gone. I thought that when I got back we would resume recording the song "Like Honey" for Michael G., but no. They had already completed the song with Matt singing the verses and with the songwriters doing all the background vocals. Since Auto-Tune was now popular, it fit well with Matt's vocals. I honestly didn't like the song and not because I wasn't on it. I was happy that Matt could step up and record the song, but I felt like it was done maliciously.

Three nights after I had been back in Atlanta, Teresa called us all down to a small dark room in the basement of the house. This room was only lit by a small light bulb which made the mood a bit scary. It was like an interrogation scene in an old Italian gangster film. We all sat in folding chairs in a circle and she asked us one by one, "Do you trust me?"

While Matt and Kev gave her the obvious "I'm going to tell you what you want to hear answer", I gave her the truth. I told her, "No, I don't trust you."

By that point Teresa had manipulated, lied, abused, and pimped me and I had lost all respect and trust for her. I then realized that she was doing this to benefit her desire of being in control. She controlled all of us with fear. She had an individual tactic that she used for her control, and it worked.

Even with her own son she used the situation with his dad to control him. She would tell him that his father left them because of him. No son wants to hear that from their mother.

When I told her, "No, I don't trust you," she looked at me as if she was going to burn a hole straight through my heart. The other guys in the group kept silent and looked directly at me as if I was a slave that just spit in the face of his master. The tension in the dark room felt heavy. It was a thick, cold, lonely, deathly dark feeling that you could almost taste. I felt like we were about to call on some evil spirits. Indeed I was dealing with evil spirits but it didn't scare me anymore.

While all eyes were on me, I felt powerful. I felt like I was taking back everything that I had allowed Teresa to have and that was my trust. I trusted her with my dreams and my life. I was now in control and I can tell Teresa truly hated me for it. Outside of her own son, I was the first to stand up to her. To be honest, whenever the rest of the guys would sit and discuss how bad Teresa was amongst each other, I rarely chimed in. I would just sit and listen to all they had to say because I wanted to see if they felt the same way I was feeling. I wasn't raised to be fearful of people but somehow I welcomed it when it came to Teresa. She was very powerful but I didn't care. The worst thing she could do is kill me, and I was no longer afraid.

First meeting Teresa you would think she's the most caring, giving, and respectful person but these were just some of the characteristics she used to wheel people in. She used her material possessions as a way to gain respect and power from others. Teresa was a psychologist at one point in her life, so she knew how the human psyche works. She was the master of manipulation. She could get you to believe things about yourself that aren't true. She also loved being the center of attention.

Even though "Last Horizon" was the main focus for me and the guys, she always made it about her. She knew how to pick at our insecurities to get us to do what she wanted.

She secretively knew about my sexuality from Maestro and always used it against me. If she felt like I was getting too confident she'd say things like, "I got an email today from one of the record executives saying that you're gay and they have photographic proof of it."

Even though I knew that had to be a lie there were parts of me that actually believed her. I knew I didn't take any photos that would jeopardize mine or the groups' reputation. She knew that my sexuality may have been something that I was indeed a bit sensitive about and to control me she used that weapon all the time.

There was this one instance where we did a show and fans, radio personalities, record execs, and others were all saying that I'm indeed the star of Last Horizon. Teresa then came to me later that day saying that a gay guy approached her saying that he had slept with me and had threaten to go to bloggers and expose my sexuality.

To be completely honest, my sexuality has NEVER been a secret. I wasn't forthcoming with my personal affairs but if someone was to ever ask me in a respectable way I was always honest about it. Even though at the times when I was a bit embarrassed, I still had the courage to tell the truth. People may feel like I was living a lie but, if you never ask me I will never tell you.

When it came to the group and Teresa, I wanted to tell them, just so that they would be aware of it all. I felt like I was going to spend my entire life being a part of Last Horizon at the time, so they deserved to know who I was. But knowing who I was just helped Teresa control me.

When I got to my room after our dark meeting, I knew I couldn't live in that house another night. Now that Teresa knew how I really felt about her she was going to make my life hell. I felt like if I didn't leave I was giving her permission to kill me. To save my own life I had to take a chance and get out of there.

I texted Marcel and asked if I could stay with him for a while. He said that he would be happy to help me as much as he could. I didn't want to pull anyone else into my drama with Teresa, but I needed to get away. After everyone was sleeping that night I begin to pack a few of my things. I took everything that was important. I didn't want to take a lot because I didn't want to get caught leaving the house.

I even left my phone sitting on my bed. I didn't want any calls from Teresa or anybody that's involved with Last Horizon. I wasn't expecting to hear from my family back home until my Birthday which was only two days away. But I planned to have another phone by then to call them and let them know that I was okay.

I was extremely nervous because if I got caught I'm not sure what Teresa would try to do to me. I quietly snuck out of the back door and walked around to the front of the house to my car. I sat in the car and was scared to start it up because I didn't want any one in the house to hear me. I left the car door open, put it in neutral, and steered backwards down the long drive way. I was so nervous that I began to sweat a lot. It was now or never, there's no way I could turn back. When I reached the end of the drive way I started my car and quickly put it in drive. I didn't turn on my headlights until I was on the highway. I did close to 90 mph all the way to Marcel's house.

Thankfully there were no police out that night. The whole drive, I felt free. I felt like I could get back to my old self for a while. Everything that I had accomplished with Last Horizon was now history and I refused to look back. I had planned to reach out to Michael G. in a few weeks. I was hoping that things would have blown over by then.

TRACK 21:
Ain't No Sunshine

When I got to Marcel's house, he welcomed me in and gave me a blanket. He told me I could sleep on his couch. He sat in the living room with me for a while as I explained to him everything that was going on. He welcomed me to stay as long as I needed to. I thought that David would be there with him but he wasn't.

"Where's David?" I asked.

"David was rushed to the hospital from work a day ago," he said.

"Is he okay?" I asked concernedly.

"He had a hard time breathing the other day. He'll be in the hospital for a while. I went up to see him earlier today but he was sleeping. The medication the doctors have him on makes him drowsy," he said.

I've never seen David with even a cold. I'm not sure how to take him laying in a hospital bed battling HIV.

The very next day I went to buy a prepaid cell phone so that I could call my family back home in Illinois. I told my mother everything that was happening with me, the group and Teresa. This was the first time I was completely honest to my mother about what was really going on. I usually made it seem as if everything was going great when it came to the group. She of course was very worried and urged me to come home as soon as possible.

After speaking with my mother I went up to the hospital to see David. He was very happy to see me. His room was ice cold and smelled like hospital food. His bed was facing a window with a view of a pond with multi-colored flowers around it. This view was extremely peaceful and hypnotizing. David seemed to be in good spirits but very weak. We talked for about an hour as he dozed on and off.

"I'm getting out of here tomorrow, I'll be home, sweet home," he said, smiling.

"Yes, you are. On my birthday, too! We have to go out," I laughed.

"That's right! I was going to call you to surprise you. But since you're here Happy early Birthday to you," he laughed and started to cough.

"Thanks. I really hope you feel better David," I said slowly.

"I will... I'll be just fine. I hope you feel better too. Thank you, Juan." he said as he slowly dozed off.

"Thank me for what", I asked laughing. I turned to gaze out the window at the pond waiting for a response. I looked back at him and noticed that he had dozed off.

The nurse then came in and told me I had to leave while they changed his IV and to give him some rest. By the looks of it, David wasn't coming home tomorrow. I didn't want to leave the hospital because I had a strong feeling that this could be the last time I would see David. He didn't look good at all. He almost looked like a completely different person. He had lost lots of weight and looked over-tired. I couldn't believe this was David. Wow.

I went downstairs in the waiting area and stayed there daydreaming for about three hours before I finally left. Even though David and I had been broken up for over a year, I still loved him.

When I got back to Marcel's house I felt so empty. I knew that I couldn't stay there too long, even though he said I could stay as long as I wanted. I planned to go back home to Illinois the day after my birthday. I didn't want to tell David that I had planned to leave Atlanta. I knew he was going through enough already. I didn't want to worry him with my problems.

The next day was my birthday and though I was happy to be alive for another year there was a lot on my mind. I could barely sleep at night because I was so paranoid that Teresa would have someone find me. I would have nightmares of someone sneaking in my room at night and setting me on fire. I was constantly looking over my shoulder. I thought the only way for me to get over this was to leave Atlanta and return home.

I went to the hospital to see David and when I arrived to his room the bed was empty. I immediately went to the nurse at the desk to ask her if he had gone home. She told me that David had died earlier that morning. Whoa. I could not believe this. I cried the hardest I have ever cried in my life. I thought I took my father's death hard but this hurt even more.

I've always heard of superstitions like "Death happens in threes". In such a short time I have lost three people that were close in my life. Death seemed to linger around me and I truly felt like I would be next. The nurse and two others guided me to the waiting area. They told me that David's parents have already come and gone. I knew Marcel was at work at the time so I doubted if he knew already. Instead of calling him to tell him, I thought it would be best if I went up to his job to see him.

When I got to Marcel's job I went inside to see him there crying. Without a word, I just hugged him. I guess he had found out earlier. Once we both stopped crying he did explain to me that David actually had AIDS. He said that David didn't want me to know. He felt that I took it hard enough knowing he was HIV positive.

My birthday went from being a day I loved to celebrate to a day that I dreaded. I started to really feel like none of this would have happened if I didn't join the group. Everything in my life was crumbling and now I was in fear of my own life as well.

I decided to leave Atlanta the night of David's memorial service which was a week later. I felt like I was burying my dreams, my love, and the past. David is someone that I will always cherish. I have never loved someone so much, and doubt I ever will again.

I honestly didn't know what was going on in the press at the time about the group. I didn't watch television or check anything on the internet. I could imagine that fans were still in shock over Cal's death. By that point I didn't want to return to music period. I had had enough and my time to shine was over.

TRACK 22:
Livin' On A Prayer

After being home for about three months, I began to miss singing again. Since I had been through so much in the past year I wanted to sing about those things. I bought some studio equipment and set it up at my mother's house and began to work on a new project. My album titled, "The Reason Why I Sing".

This was an inspirational album that I wanted to release independently. I wrote and recorded all the songs and it felt good to create again. After I allowed my mom and some other family members to hear my new work, they really felt like I should try to get back into the music industry. They really felt like, "Reason Why I Sing" would be something special for my fans and the music industry.

After contemplating the idea for weeks, I remembered the conversation I had with Michael G. So I reached out to him and he was surprised and shocked to hear from me. He promised that he wouldn't tell Teresa that he had spoken to me. He said that he hadn't heard from Teresa in over a month. He also told me that he ended up dropping Last Horizon from Hit Maker Records. Apparently Teresa found a replacement for me but Michael G. decided that the group's stability and sell potential wasn't worth the investment. He demanded Teresa to return the money he released to her in which she didn't. I wasn't surprised by anything he told me regarding Teresa. No matter who she replaced me with; Last Horizon will never rise to the top. Not because of the guys but because of Teresa.

I told him about the album that I recorded and he was interested in hearing it. I emailed him the songs for my album and he loved it. He wanted to fly me to New York so that I could re-record it in a better

studio and with some of his producers, in which I did.

When I got to New York, it felt good but brought back way too

many bad memories. Michael G. was really different this time around. He

seemed to be way more interested in my music than anything else which

made me immediately comfortable.

Initially I was supposed to stay in the same hotel were Cal died,

but I was very adamant about not staying there. I just didn't want to

relive anything. Michael G. put me up in another expensive hotel which

was several blocks away from the studio and Hit Maker Records' office.

I was set up to stay in the hotel until I completed the album and

was able to establish new management. Even though I was still under

contract with Teresa as my manager, Michael G. was confident that she

wouldn't try to sue me. Teresa was going to do everything but go to a

courthouse. She also knew I knew way too much about her personal life

to allow me the opportunity to say it to a judge.

The recording process for my album was going great. Michael G. was extremely supportive of me and my ideas for my album. I was able to collaborate with Nicky on my album as well as hers. My and Nicky's relationship had become a bit more serious during the recording phase of this album. She was there for every session just to support me.

Because I had just been through so much in my life, she listened to me talk about it all for hours. She never judged, just listened and comforted me when I needed it. For the final track on my album, I wrote a title song called "Reason Why I Sing". This song was my new anthem. It spoke of all the things I've been through with my father, David, the group, and friendships. It really spelled out the reason why I sing.

I had just finished recording "Reason Why I Sing", it was late at night so I left the studio and headed to the hotel. I got an eerie feeling like someone was watching me. I could feel their eyes on the back of my neck. I turned a few times to look around just to make sure nothing was there. I thought maybe I was starting to get paranoid again. When I got upstairs and opened my room door, I went inside.

I was waiting to hear my room door shut behind me but it didn't. I felt a strong blunt force hit me on the back of my head and I fell to the floor. I quickly turned around to see a big guy in all black with a ski mask on. He reached down and grabbed me tightly by the neck. My heart pounded uncontrollably as he pointed a hand gun directly between my eyes. He was choking me so hard with his bare hands that I couldn't breathe. My life flashed before my eyes all in a few seconds. I had seen every good and bad moments of my life.

I knew this guy had to have been sent here by Teresa. There was something eerily familiar about him. His eyes looked as if I seen them before, as well as the ugly tattoo on his hand. But how did she know I was here? Wow, was this it for me? He looked me dead in the eye as I looked down the barrel of the gun and said, "Now here's your reason to sing."

I closed my eyes and my world went silent...

REASON WHY I SING

-Mike Spears

To Be Continued...

BONUS TRACK:

Reason Why I Sing

Hold on; let me talk to God for a moment...

Thank You God for life, experience, understanding, patience, strength, success, growth, my family, friends, acquaintances, my gifts, and talents. Thank you for putting this story in my spirit and allowing me the task of writing it. I trust your promise that all will be well and I vow to continue to be strong through it all. Bless those that took time to read this story. Bless them with the courage and strength to free themselves from the bondage that's been place upon them by man. God, bless this story to reach the hearts and the minds of the hopeless. Bless this story to be received and used for the purpose of love. God I would like to thank you in advance for the great things you're going to do in my future. Amen.

Okay, back to you...

I would like to thank you again for taking time out of your busy life to read Reason Why I Sing. This book is dedicated to anybody who has ever felt ashamed of who they were or what they did in their past. What you did is in the past. Forgive yourself and live in your truth. You owe it to yourself to be free. Free from self petty, guilt, shame and hatred. You owe yourself happiness. Most of all, you owe yourself LOVE.

Writing this book has been a therapeutic experience for me. I've been able to tell a lot of my life story through the character of Juan. Naming myself Juan in the story gave me a sense of freedom to write some of the most shameful events that occurred in my life. During the writing process I depended on Juan to be my voice. I wanted him to be my reflection. Sometimes it's hard to see exactly where we go wrong or even admit to it because we can only see from our own perspectives. By writing through Juan I've been able to see exactly where I caused pain and conflict. I can now take complete ownership of my mistakes. Yes, I was dealing with some dirty people but I allowed them to make me just as dirty.

When I came to the end of this story I wanted a way to free myself from that character. Killing Juan was a symbolic way of me killing that person I used to be. For literary reasons I allowed this story to end with a suspenseful cliff hanger because I wanted to set the REASON WHY I SING series in motion. I based this first part of this series on my own life with hopes of helping other people understand the crazy life of entertainers. I wanted people to realize that people you see on TV i.e. singers, actors, preachers, news anchors, talk show host and reality stars all have a real story. No one's' life has been as perfect as many may try to paint it out to seem.

In order for me to live the rest of my life as I've imagined it, I knew I would have to release myself. I had to break loose from the torment I allowed myself to bare from other's opinions. I'm now a lot more confident, stronger, braver, wiser, happier, and free which is the Reason Why I Sing.

Love Ya'll.

-Mike Spears

Coming Soon By Mike Spears

BOY X

One night stands may seem cliché in today's society. But what happens when a one night stand turns into a life time of regret? We quickly learn that what looks good may not be good for us at all. Alan an award winning photographer finds himself in the War of Love, struggling to get back to where love first began. Being trapped in emotions that may only be cured by death. This drama filled series will have you on the edge of your seat, mouth wide open, in total disbelief as the story unfolds itself.

"I wrote the story of Boy X because I wanted something fresh while I worked on part two of Reason Why I Sing. I wanted a story that was intense, passionate, crazy, sexy, suspenseful and REAL", says Mike Spears. The story thickens like molasses as each character reveals the Boy X within. This series is the type of story that people will gossip about at the salon or barber shops. The characters are easy to follow and read because they all come from a place where we've all been; hurt, and deceived. Stayed tuned for the official release date.

Discussion Questions:

Here are some questions that you can ask your friends or even yourself.

1. Which is worse, failing or never trying?
2. Would you lie to God? If not, why do we lie to people? Are they more important than God?
3. Why do religions that support love cause so many wars?
4. What would you do differently if you knew nobody would judge you?
5. Will you date someone that you knew was HIV positive?
6. Why are you, you?
7. Will you date a friend's ex?
8. Have you been the kind of friend you want as a friend?
9. They say everyone has a price. What's your price?
10. What is success to you?
11. What is the one thing you'd most like to change about the world?
12. If you knew that everyone you know was going to die tomorrow, who would you visit today?
13. What would you do differently if you knew nobody would judge you?
14. If we learn from our mistakes, why are we always so afraid to make a mistake?
15. What's the Reason Why YOU Sing?

Join Me Online:

ITSMIKESPEARS.COM

Facebook.com/AuthorMikeSpears

Twitter.com/itsmikespears

Instagram.com/itsmikespears

Ask.fm/itsmikespears

www.ingramcontent.com/pod-product-compliance
Lightning Source LLC
Chambersburg PA
CBHW060056150626
46556CB00017BA/915